A human guinea pig . . .

"It seems to me that we have plenty of interesting suggestions about ways to scare the boys," Janet said. "I think we should try some of them out first."

The girls looked at each other. "Try them on who?" Amy asked.

"We need a guinea pig," Janet explained. "A human guinea pig that we can test these scares out on."

"It sounds OK to me," Maria said. "But where do we find a guinea pig?"

At that moment, a dreadful noise came floating up the stairs. "What on earth is that?" Janet asked, clamping her hands across her ears.

"That," Jessica sighed, "is our so-called brother."

"It's Johnny Buck," Elizabeth put in. "He thinks he's singing Johnny's new song, 'Gotcha,' but he can't sing on key."

"'Gonna getcha, gonna getcha . . .'" Mandy sang along. She shook her head sadly. "Too bad. It's such a great song. 'Gonna getcha, looked gonna getcha.'"

"Gotcha!" Janet yelled, suddenly jumping up.

Elizabeth smothered a grin. The other girls stared. Janet didn't often lose her composure, even over Johnny Buck.

When she saw everyone staring at her, Janet cleared her throat. "What I mean is, Steven's the one," she said, her voice now calm. "

SWEET VALLEY TWINS

Steven
Gets
Even

Written by
Jamie Suzanne

Created by
FRANCINE PASCAL

BANTAM BOOKS
NEW YORK · TORONTO · LONDON · SYDNEY · AUCKLAND

RL 4, 008-012

STEVEN GETS EVEN
A Bantam Book / July 1995

Sweet Valley High® *and Sweet Valley Twins*™ *are*
registered trademarks of Francine Pascal

Conceived by Francine Pascal

Produced by Daniel Weiss Associates, Inc.
33 West 17th Street
New York, NY 10011

Cover art by James Mathewuse

ISBN: 0-553-48189-4

Published simultaneously in the United States and Canada

Bantam Books are published by Bantam Books, a division of Bantam
Doubleday Dell Publishing Group, Inc. Its trademark, consisting of the
words "Bantam Books" and the portrayal of a rooster, is Registered in the
U.S. Patent and Trademark Office and in other countries. Marca
Registrada. Bantam Books, 1540 Broadway, New York, New York 10036.

PRINTED IN THE UNITED STATES OF AMERICA

OPM   0 9 8 7 6 5 4 3 2 1

To Meris Rose Tombari

One

"All right, guys, it's trivia time," Mr. Bowman said during English class on Tuesday afternoon. "Anyone want to tell us what Frankenstein looks like?"

Elizabeth Wakefield looked around at her classmates. Hands were shooting up all over the room. In front of her, Charlie Cashman was practically bouncing out of his seat as he waved his arm wildly in the air.

"Seems like a popular question," Mr. Bowman observed. "All right, Charlie. Describe Frankenstein for us, please."

"He's a monster," Charlie blurted out. "He's fierce and bloodthirsty, and he walks kind of like this." Charlie stood up and took a few lumbering steps to demonstrate. Elizabeth rolled her eyes.

"Nice try, Charlie," Mr. Bowman said, smiling.

"But I'm afraid you haven't quite gotten it. Someone else?"

Hands waved again. Turning around, Elizabeth could see her twin sister, Jessica, leaning back in her seat with her hand up. Jessica looked exactly like Elizabeth, with bluish-green eyes, long blond hair, and a dimple in her left cheek. But similar as they were on the outside, the Wakefield twins were very different people.

Jessica was a member of an exclusive club called the Unicorn Club, which was made up of the prettiest and most popular girls at Sweet Valley Middle School. Most of her energy went toward club meetings and activities, and like the other members of the Unicorn Club, she was mainly interested in boys, clothes, and gossip.

Elizabeth was the more serious and studious twin. She loved to curl up with a good book, and she spent many hours working on the class newspaper, *The Sweet Valley Sixers*. Her friends weren't as popular as Jessica's, but she considered them a lot more fun. Privately, she called Jessica and her fellow Unicorns "the Snob Squad."

Mr. Bowman noticed Jessica's raised hand and called on her.

Jessica cleared her throat. "Frankenstein has a square head," she began in a dramatic voice. She drew a huge square in the air with her finger. "And there are little bits of black hair that don't really cover his forehead." She started sketching them in.

"Thanks, Jessica, but that's not quite right, either," Mr. Bowman said, interrupting her. He looked around the room once more. "Brian? How about you?"

Brian Boyd, who was sitting next to Charlie, thrust his chair back. "He's got these big scars all over his face," he said, indicating where with his fingers. "It's really gross. It's like he cut himself shaving or something."

"It's like he was shaving with a chain saw," Charlie added, starting to snicker. Elizabeth rolled her eyes once again. She wrote "BOYS!!!" on a piece of paper, added a face with a tongue sticking out, and showed it to her friend Amy Sutton.

"Thanks, Charlie," Mr. Bowman said pleasantly, "but you've already had your turn. Sorry, Brian. The real Frankenstein doesn't have scars all over his face—and he certainly wouldn't shave with a chain saw."

Amy leaned over and wrote "You are so right!" next to Elizabeth's picture.

"Anyone else?" Mr. Bowman asked.

Elizabeth thought hard. What had she read about Frankenstein? She raised her hand. "I think Frankenstein wasn't a monster," she said slowly. "Wasn't he really a young man instead?" She snapped her fingers. "Frankenstein was the scientist who created the monster and brought him to life, right?"

Mr. Bowman grinned. "That's correct. Very good, Elizabeth. Not many grown-ups know who

Frankenstein really is. Try it out on your parents to-night." He picked up a book and came around to the front of his desk. "Anyway, I asked you that question because we're going to be spending the next couple of weeks studying one of my favorite topics—scary books."

The room exploded into conversation. Elizabeth flashed Amy an excited grin.

Mr. Bowman quieted the class. "Today I want to spend the rest of the period reading from *Frankenstein*—not the movie, but the book, which was written by Mary Shelley in 1817."

"*Frankenstein* was written by a woman?" Elizabeth asked, surprised and a little proud at the same time.

Brian Boyd swiveled around to face her. "It must not be any good, then," he said, just loud enough for her to hear. Elizabeth made a face at him. *Boys!*

Mr. Bowman nodded. "How *Frankenstein* came to be written is a story in itself," he said, crossing to the classroom door and switching off the lights. His voice dropped to just above a whisper as he came back and perched on the edge of his desk. "Late one night, Mary and several of her friends were sitting around a fire. They were telling ghost stories. Anyone here ever done that?"

Elizabeth's hand shot up. She caught Amy's eye. In the gloom of the classroom, Elizabeth felt a little shiver run down her spine. She'd told ghost stories, all right!

Mr. Bowman smiled at the forest of hands in front of him. "I thought so," he said. "Anyway, one of Mary's friends challenged them all to write their own ghost stories. They accepted the challenge. You know how you have due dates for your school assignments? Well, they had a deadline, too."

"What was the deadline?" Elizabeth asked, curious.

"A year," Mr. Bowman replied.

"No fair!" Charlie Cashman burst out, standing halfway out of his chair. "How come you never give us a year on our homework?"

"Charlie," Mr. Bowman said, lifting up his copy of *Frankenstein*, "this book is three hundred and twenty pages long. The next time I assign you to write a three-hundred-twenty-page essay for school, I promise I'll give you a year to write it." Charlie slumped down in his seat, looking embarrassed. Elizabeth couldn't help snickering.

"A couple of days later," Mr. Bowman continued, leaning forward, "Mary got started on her story. Lots of times, writers go out and get ideas for their books. That didn't happen to Mary. Instead, the idea found her." His voice got softer and softer and more and more ominous. Elizabeth strained to hear. There was a nervous feeling in the pit of her stomach.

"She had a dream one night," Mr. Bowman went on after a pause. "She dreamed of a horrifying monster. When she woke up, she was relieved to find she'd only been dreaming. But the image of the monster wouldn't go away."

Elizabeth shivered. She began to wish Mr. Bowman would talk a little louder. She stole a quick look around the room. *It's just an ordinary Tuesday afternoon*, she told herself.

Of course, on ordinary Tuesday afternoons, the class was much noisier.

Mr. Bowman sat up straight. "Then Mary Shelley said to herself, 'What terrified me will terrify others.' That night she began to write. And by the end of the year, she was the only member of her little group to have finished a story. The name of the story?" Mr. Bowman pointed at the book in his hand. "*Frankenstein*."

Elizabeth shivered again. Was that a clap of thunder? She checked outside. No, the sky was bright, the sun was shining down. She was just imagining things.

Mr. Bowman jumped up suddenly and began to pace around the room. "I'll warn you right now," he said. "Don't say I never gave you any advice. Some of the stories we read may be a little bit scary." He stopped near Jessica's desk at the back of the room and whirled to face the class. "You also have an assignment," he told them. "You must read a spooky story yourself over the next two weeks and report on it to the class. You can do a regular book report, a story of your own based on the characters, a diorama, a poster . . . whatever you want.

But there's one restriction—the book you choose has to be over twenty years old."

"Who wants to read old writers?" Jessica scoffed. "That stuff's not scary."

Even Amy rolled her eyes. "Kids today are too sophisticated to be frightened by a story like *Frankenstein*, Mr. Bowman," she told the teacher.

"Yeah! What about one of those books with vampires that chew off people's heads?" Brian asked. "Now *that's* scary!"

Mr. Bowman smiled at the class and walked back to the front of the room. "You might find that these 'old' writers are a little more frightening than you think."

"No way," Jessica piped up from the back of the room. "I don't care what Mary Shelley dreamed about, it won't possibly frighten kids like us."

"The world's changed, Mr. Bowman," Jessica's friend Lila Fowler chimed in. "They show bloody stuff all the time on TV now. Next to that, *Frankenstein* sounds pretty tame. I mean, is there a lot of blood in it?"

Mr. Bowman looked thoughtful. "No, there isn't, Lila, but—"

"Then it can't be all that scary," Jessica said, interrupting, and she pretended to yawn.

"She's right, Mr. Bowman," Elizabeth added. "Kids today grow up a lot faster than they used to. Those stories are going to be a lot of fun, but scary? No way. They might frighten a third-grader, but we're much more mature than that." *Well, most of us are*, she added to herself, looking at Charlie and Brian. *With a few notable exceptions.*

Mr. Bowman shook his head slowly. "Pictures aren't always as scary as words. Stories can sometimes pack a wallop that you might not expect. And the things that seem the most familiar, the most ordinary—sometimes they can actually be the scariest."

"Not for us," Jessica argued. "Not for me, anyway."

Mr. Bowman looked directly at Jessica and grinned. Elizabeth wasn't at all sure she liked the looks of that grin. "Are you sure about that, Jessica?" he asked softly.

Once again, the class became very quiet. Elizabeth swallowed hard. She could hear the hum of the clock in the darkened room. It felt almost as if there were a chill in the air. But Jessica didn't hesitate. "Sure I'm sure," she said. "They won't scare me."

Out of the corner of her eye, Elizabeth saw Charlie and Brian look at each other. Their mouths began to curve up into smiles as Mr. Bowman spoke. "All right, Jessica," he said. "Have it your way. I'll talk to you again in two weeks." He opened the large book to a page somewhere near the middle and began to read aloud.

"Girls! It's dinnertime!" Mrs. Wakefield, the twins' mother, called to them on Tuesday night.

Jessica came into the dining room, still thinking about English class that afternoon. "Hey, Mom," she asked, sliding into her seat, "do you know what Frankenstein looks like?"

"Frankenstein?" Mrs. Wakefield looked puzzled. "He's a monster, isn't he? A big square head, some missing teeth, a scar across his face." She passed Jessica the salad bowl.

"Gotcha!" Jessica said triumphantly, taking a few leaves of lettuce and covering them with ranch dressing. "You're wrong. Think about it."

"Take a little more salad and maybe I will," her mother suggested. "You've got enough dressing on your plate for three people."

Jessica sighed and stabbed four more lettuce leaves with her fork. "So who was Frankenstein?" she asked again just as Elizabeth and Steven, the twins' fourteen-year-old brother, entered the dining room.

"Frankenstein lives in this house," Steven announced. "I'm looking right at her." He stared intently into Jessica's face.

Jessica glared at him and held up her fork warningly. "Maybe we'll have Steven chops instead of lamb chops tonight," she said, wishing Steven would go live in one of Mary Shelley's novels. "Anyway, for the millionth time, who was Frankenstein?"

Mr. Wakefield rubbed his chin thoughtfully. "I think I remember." He picked up his knife and began slicing his chop. "Wasn't Frankenstein really the—"

Steven set down his glass of milk with a thud. "It was the mad scientist," he interrupted. "Everybody thinks it's the monster, but it's really the scientist."

Jessica felt her cheeks turning red. "Steven Wakefield!" she said, half rising from her chair. "I wasn't asking you!"

"But I answered," Steven pointed out, grinning. "You asked a question, and I answered it. What's wrong with that?"

"Because—" Jessica thought. "Because I wasn't asking you."

Mr. Wakefield raised his palm. "OK, kids," he told them. "That's enough. Was that the right answer, Jessica?"

"Yes," Jessica admitted grudgingly.

"How did you know about that?" Mrs. Wakefield asked.

"Oh, it came up in English class today," she said vaguely, not looking at her sister.

"I read about it somewhere," Elizabeth said. "It's really neat, Mom. We're going to be studying scary stories."

Mr. Wakefield raised his eyebrows. "Like *Frankenstein*?"

"Yeah," Jessica said in as bored a voice as she could manage. "If you can call it a scary story."

"What do you mean by that?" her mother asked.

"Well," Jessica said, shrugging. "It's really pretty tame, if you want to know the truth."

"Really?" Mr. Wakefield asked, setting down his glass. "I haven't read *Frankenstein* in years, but as I remember, it was pretty chilling." He chuckled. "Did you get to the part where the monster comes to life?"

Jessica jumped. That was the first part Mr. Bowman had read aloud. And actually, it had seemed scary back then—well, a little bit scary, anyway. But that was only because Mr. Bowman knew how to put on a spooky voice.

"That part? Oh, that part was pretty lame, Dad," Jessica said, looking across at Elizabeth for support.

Elizabeth nodded, slowly at first and then more vigorously. "It wasn't scary at all compared to the stuff they're writing now."

Mr. Wakefield cocked an eyebrow. "I don't know. Have you ever read any Poe?"

"You mean Edgar Alvin Poe?" Jessica asked.

"Edgar *Allan* Poe," Elizabeth corrected her. "Some of his stories are on the suggested reading list Mr. Bowman gave us today."

"Alvin, Allan, who cares?" Jessica asked.

Steven gave her a look. "Jessica, Mess-ica, who cares?" he teased her. His mouth was full of milk, and a little bit dripped down his chin.

Jessica turned away in disgust. She looked at her sister and pointed to Steven. "Now, *that's* scary, Lizzie, wouldn't you agree?" she asked.

Elizabeth smiled and nodded as Mr. Wakefield opened his mouth to speak again. "Jessica," he said, wagging his forefinger at her, "don't tell me how tame those 'old' stories are till you've read some of Poe's work."

"Oh, come on," Jessica scoffed. "How scary could he be?"

"Your voice is awfully loud, Jessica," Mrs. Wakefield put in. She ground some pepper onto her baked potato. "Is there something wrong?"

"No," Jessica stated, trying to speak in a softer tone. *Was I loud?* she wondered. "Tell you what," she said. "I'll read a Poe story for my project." *Preferably a short one.* "And I bet it won't be scary at all."

Mr. and Mrs. Wakefield exchanged amused glances. "Yeah, right, Jessica," Steven muttered, spearing the last baked potato and cutting it open savagely. "Whatever you say."

"I bet it'll be pretty stupid, really," Jessica went on. "My whole report will be just nine words long: 'My brother's face is a lot scarier than this.'"

"Gee, thanks a lot," Steven muttered. He smeared a huge chunk of butter across the top of his potato.

"What's the matter?" Jessica asked innocently. "Your face would stop King Kong in his tracks. You know it would."

"Jessica," Mrs. Wakefield said quietly.

"That's another so-called scary monster," Jessica

went on, gathering steam. The nerve of her family, accusing her of being scared by things from the Dark Ages! "King Kong, Poe, Frankenstein. Baby stuff." She pointed a finger at her brother. "You don't exactly make the big leagues, either, Steven, but you've got it all over them."

"That's enough, Jessica," Mr. Wakefield said, a warning in his voice.

"It's OK, Dad," Steven said, his eyes narrowing. "She's probably acting this way because she's freaked out by *Frankenstein*, and she doesn't want to admit it."

Jessica glared at her brother. "That's the craziest—"

"I mean, I read *Frankenstein* last year," Steven interrupted. "And there were a few parts that *could* be scary—to a little sixth grader."

Jessica shifted in her chair. Steven had lowered his voice. He sounded a lot like Mr. Bowman had that afternoon in English class. Steven fixed her with his eyes. They seemed to be looking right through her.

Jerking her head away, Jessica saw both her parents smiling at her. She forced a careless laugh. "You can't scare me, either, Steven Wakefield," Jessica said as firmly as she could manage. "*Nothing* is going to scare me, either at school or at home, for at least the next two weeks!"

Two

"I think I'll pick *The Legend of Sleepy Hollow*," Amy told Elizabeth. The two girls were sitting together in Mr. Bowman's classroom just before English on Wednesday. Each girl had her reading list in front of her.

"That sounds good," Elizabeth agreed, remembering the story of how the schoolmaster Ichabod Crane met up with a Headless Horseman late one night—and was never seen again. "Did you ever see the movie?"

"The Disney one? Uh-huh," Amy said with a grin, circling the name of the book on her paper. She added a check mark next to the name of the author, Washington Irving. "Don't tell anybody, but I still like to watch it every now and then."

Elizabeth chuckled. "So do I," she confessed.

"But I don't like to watch it with no one else in the house."

Amy stared at Elizabeth. "Why not?" she asked.

Elizabeth felt her face turn red. "Oh—I don't know," she said vaguely. "It's a little bit scary, I guess. I mean, I was pretty young the last time I saw it. Probably in second grade."

"Did your parents leave you alone in the house when you were in second grade?" Amy asked, a puzzled look on her face.

"Oh—" Elizabeth began in confusion.

"Hey, guys." Maria Slater, another of Elizabeth's friends, set her book down at the desk next to Amy.

"Hi, Maria," Elizabeth said, grateful for the interruption. "So what scary book are you going to read for your project?"

"*Frankenstein*," Maria told her with a smile. "I started reading it myself last night."

"Is it creepy?" Elizabeth asked with interest, watching Maria's face.

"Not really," Maria said after a pause.

"Not really?" Elizabeth repeated.

Maria shook her head vigorously. "Not creepy at all," she said, sounding like she meant it. "I've been in commercials that were more frightening." Maria had been a child actress who had also appeared in movies.

Am I the only one around here with imagination? Elizabeth asked herself as Mr. Bowman walked by, preparing for the start of class. "Have you chosen a book yet, Elizabeth?" he asked.

"Not yet," Elizabeth admitted. "I can't seem to decide."

Mr. Bowman leaned over and took a look at Elizabeth's reading list. "Let's see," he said, tracing a line down the page with his finger. "Not that one—no—too easy—not scary enough—"

Elizabeth wasn't sure she liked the way he said "not scary enough."

"Ha!" Mr. Bowman leaned forward with excitement. "I recommend this one for you," he said, tapping a title called *The Hound of the Baskervilles*. "It's a Sherlock Holmes mystery by Arthur Conan Doyle, but it's not a short story like the others—it's a full-length novel. The writing can be a little tricky. Still, you'd probably get a kick out of it, Elizabeth. And it's pretty bloodcurdling." He stepped back, a twinkle in his eye, and howled like a dog baying at the moon. "Owoooo!"

"Oh, stop it, Mr. Bowman," Elizabeth said, embarrassed. But she had to admit, the book sounded great: mystery, animals, and fright. She only hoped there wasn't too much fright.

Jessica came into the classroom, talking excitedly with Lila and a few other Unicorns. As Jessica sat down, Elizabeth noticed Charlie and Brian gesturing frantically toward their friend Aaron Dallas, who was sitting in the other corner of the room.

Elizabeth watched them with curiosity. What were those boys up to?

And what could it have to do with Jessica?

"'There were hairs in the center of his palm,'" Mr. Bowman read from his worn copy of Bram Stoker's *Dracula* once class began. "'The nails were long and fine, and cut to a sharp point.'"

Jessica shuddered. She hadn't been planning to listen hard. But despite herself, she found herself being drawn into the story. It was much more dramatic than she'd thought.

And scarier, too.

"'The Count leaned over me and his hands touched me,'" Mr. Bowman continued. Jessica gasped and drew back in her seat.

Then the storm broke. First there was a flash of lightning. Next came a huge thunderclap. There were a few muffled screams, and Jessica found herself halfway to the floor. With a start she realized that she had been diving under her desk.

At least I didn't scream my head off, Jessica thought, getting back into her seat. *Like some people I could mention*, she added silently, staring at Lila.

"Ahh yesss," Mr. Bowman said, speaking a little louder so he could be heard over the noise of the storm. Jessica wished he wouldn't use such a dramatic voice. "Zee perfect veather for a chilling story like thisss."

It's just a story, Jessica told herself as the teacher

returned to his reading. *Isn't it fun to get the shivers?*

"'I saw Dracula's awful, sneering mouth dripping with my fresh blood!'" Mr. Bowman read, quoting the heroine of the story. *Totally fun*, Jessica told herself again. *A blast.*

She just hoped Edgar Allan Poe's stories weren't quite this much fun.

"That was pretty cool, wasn't it?" Lila asked Jessica. The girls were walking down the hallway after class along with Elizabeth, Amy, and Maria.

Jessica stole a quick look at her friend. "Oh, yeah," she agreed. "I don't know why Mr. Bowman keeps on talking about how scary these stories are, though. I mean, Dracula sounds like a teddy bear." She waved her hand in the air. "Ha, ha."

"Really," Lila agreed. "I mean, vampires aren't real, and if there *were* any vampires they'd live in Transylvania, not Sweet Valley, and besides there *aren't* any vampires. And I'm not scared of a story about things that don't exist."

"Right." Jessica dialed the combination of her locker. "It's really pouring outside, Elizabeth," she told her sister, quickly changing the subject. "Do you think we can get Mom to pick us up?"

Elizabeth frowned. "I doubt it," she said. "I think we're going to have to make a run for it."

"I'll walk with you," Amy offered.

"Me, too," Lila said.

Jessica looked around. The building was emptier

than usual for right after school. Apparently most of the other students had left as quickly as they could. "OK," she said. "But, Lizzie, don't you have to go up to the bathroom first?" There was no girls' bathroom on the first floor of Sweet Valley Middle School.

Elizabeth shook her head. "No."

"Oh," Jessica said. "Are you sure? I mean, usually you go before we leave."

Elizabeth stared at Jessica. "No, I don't," she said slowly. That wasn't the answer Jessica had hoped to hear. She looked beseechingly at her sister. Suddenly Elizabeth grinned. "Oh. I see. Sure. I'll come with you if you want," she offered.

Good old Lizzie. But Jessica still hesitated. *Was Elizabeth enough?* "It's not like I'm scared or anything," she said with a careless laugh, "but maybe you should come too, Lila." She twisted a lock of hair around her little finger.

Lila looked around at the hallway, which was by now practically empty. "Well—OK," she said.

"Great!" Jessica said brightly. Then she looked at Amy and Maria. "You guys might as well come with us—I mean, the more the merrier, right?"

Elizabeth nodded vigorously. "Yeah, now that I think about it, that's a really good idea," she told her friends.

Amy looked at Maria. "Well—" she began.

"Oh, come on," Lila interrupted. "It'll be more—fun with all five of us."

"There's nothing to be worried about," Jessica added. "It's not like there are any vampires up there or anything."

"Vampires?" Amy repeated in a strangely high-pitched voice.

"Oops," Jessica continued quickly. "Did I say 'vampires'? I didn't mean 'vampires.' I meant, um, 'campfires.' There aren't any campfires up there or anything."

Maria gave a hollow laugh. "We know what you meant, Jessica," she said. "Sure, we'll go. For fun."

At the top of the stairs, Jessica heard a sudden noise. "What's that?" she barked, flattening herself against the wall. With a gasp, all the other girls did the same thing. Jessica held her breath.

Janet Howell, an eighth grader who was president of the Unicorns, came around the corner. She stopped and stared at the twins and their friends. "Jessica? Lila? What on earth is going on?"

"Oh, hi, Janet," Jessica said quickly as she straightened up. "We're just all going to the bathroom, that's all."

"All of you?" Janet asked in a contemptuous voice.

Lila smiled nervously. "Jessica has to go, that's all. The rest of us are just keeping her company in case she gets scared. Or something."

Jessica shot Lila an angry glare. "As a matter of fact, Janet," she said lightly, "Lila could have waited downstairs till we came back, but she decided she'd feel more comfortable staying with the rest of us. And, oh, by the way, why don't you come too?" *After all*, she thought, *six would be even better than five, right?*

Janet curled her upper lip. "You can't use the bathroom up here," she said dryly. "It's out of order. Flooding or something. Probably one of those little sixth graders who thinks she owns the Middle School." She looked pointedly at Jessica.

Jessica would normally have been offended by Janet's comment, but the only part she could think of was *It's out of order.*

"I guess you'll have to use the one on the third floor, Jess," Elizabeth sighed. Jessica thought she heard relief in her sister's voice. "We'll wait for you down here."

Jessica turned pale. *Use the little out-of-the-way bathroom on the third floor?* she thought. *All by myself?* Even on the brightest days, the third floor was always dark and gloomy. *There are probably spiders up there*, she thought with alarm. *Big spiders. Humongous bloodsucking spiders.*

Turning to Elizabeth, Jessica put her hand comfortingly on her twin's arm. "It's OK, Lizzie," she said, patting Elizabeth's sleeve. "If you don't want to come with me, it's really all right." She paused meaningfully and raised her voice a notch. "If you're too scared after hearing Mr. Bowman read *Dracula*, it's OK. I won't tell anyone how frightened you are."

"What are you talking about?" Elizabeth replied indignantly.

Jessica hid a smile. "Oh, nothing," she said innocently. "I mean, we all know you're not as brave as some of us . . ." She let her voice trail off.

Lila smirked. "That's right, Elizabeth," she said. "Some people are just scaredy-cats and some aren't, that's all there is to it."

Elizabeth set her jaw. "I'm not a scaredy-cat," she insisted. "I'll come with you, Jess. And so will Amy and Maria, I bet." She glanced at Lila. "Of course," she added, turning back to Jessica, "we'll probably have to leave Lila waiting here—all by herself."

"Me?" Lila squealed. Her smirk vanished.

"Well, if you're not brave enough . . ." Elizabeth began.

"Of course I'm brave enough!" Lila protested. She took a step forward. "I'm coming too."

"Yuck," Jessica said, pointing to some peeling paint on the third floor. As if on cue, the thunder rolled again.

The hallway seemed deserted. Even though five other girls were with her, Jessica couldn't remember ever feeling so jumpy and alone. "Don't make me be the last one!" Amy insisted, darting inside the bathroom on Jessica's heels. The girls huddled in the middle of the room, waiting for Jessica.

"Is that everybody?" Elizabeth asked, counting noses.

A moment later, Jessica came out of the stall and washed her hands. *We did it*, she thought proudly. *Nothing to be afraid of.*

Then the door swung open. Jessica watched in horror: an unearthly-looking hand was reaching in! *It looks almost like King Kong's!* Jessica thought with horror. But she didn't have long to study it. The lights flickered. And a moment later, there was nothing but blackness.

Uh-oh. Jessica sucked in her breath. She reached for the nearest person and grabbed what might have been a sweater—or was it the furry skin of a monster? With a gasp she let it go. A hand fluttered in front of her face. A hand—or maybe a bat! Yelling, Jessica dropped to the ground and hid her head in her hands.

At that moment Jessica heard a thunderclap, followed immediately by the sound of breaking glass. The noise echoed and reechoed in her ears as she crouched on the floor of the bathroom. Around her she could hear the screams of the other girls. One of them sounded especially familiar.

Her own.

I have to get out of here! Jessica thought. It sounded as if there were more screams now—more even than the six girls could account for. She straightened up, only to bump her head on something heavy. *It's coming to get me!* she thought at first, only to hear another voice in her head saying "It's only the sink, Jessica, it's only the sink."

Reaching out with her arms, Jessica pushed herself back away from whatever it was. Her fingers grabbed at the side. *Yes, it was only the sink*, she told herself, beginning to sob. It occurred to her that maybe it was a vampire cleverly pretending to be a sink, but she refused to let herself think about that any further.

On her way backwards, Jessica bumped another body. She reached out with one hand and caught a wrist. A scream resounded in her ear. "Let go! Let go! I don't want to die!"

Not a monster. Not a vampire, Jessica told herself firmly. *A friend.* She couldn't stop screaming long enough to say who she was, but she pulled the other girl toward the bathroom door.

What if it's locked? she thought, beginning to panic. *What if there's a gigantic spider behind it?* At that moment, something else bumped into Jessica. It felt like the hand of a mummy. Jessica screamed, louder than before—and fell hard against the bathroom door.

The door! Quickly Jessica scrambled to her knees and yanked on the handle. The hallway was dark, too, but enough light shone through the windows to make it seem bright. Compared to the bathroom, it was like heaven. Jessica collapsed to the floor. No one was in sight—no spiders, no vampires, no monsters, no mummies. *Safe at last.*

In the next instant, the other girls scrambled through the the door into the hall, landing in a heap on the floor.

"What was it?" Maria cried, still trembling as she picked herself up from the pile of girls.

"I don't know," Elizabeth said, shivering, as she, too, stood up. "It couldn't have been a vampire—*could it?*"

Lila was still sobbing. "I don't know," she whimpered. "It was like—it was like there was some *creature* or something."

"Probably my sweater," Elizabeth said rationally, though her voice shook a little. "Someone kept grabbing it."

Jessica's heart was still beating out of control. "Did anyone else see a hand reach in just before the lights went out?" she demanded, her voice squeaking with the tension.

The other girls shook their heads. "And what was the sound of that breaking glass?" Jessica asked. She was afraid to look around. *Was it a window?* she wondered. *Or something else?*

"I don't know," Lila whimpered again. She clutched Janet's shoulder tightly. Jessica noticed that even Janet looked pale and drained. "I just want to go home."

Amy nodded. "Good idea."

"Shouldn't we report this to someone?" Jessica argued.

"Report what?" Janet asked. "Report vampires

on the third floor? No one would believe us, you know. And even if they did, what then? Are they going to put vampires in detention?"

"I just think—" Jessica was about to say more, when she heard something that sounded familiar. "Listen! What's that?"

Lila screamed once more and buried her face in Janet's lap. Amy and Elizabeth clutched each other. "Wait!" Jessica commanded. "That sound isn't a vampire." *Or a spider or a monster or a werewolf*, she added to herself. *Or King Kong.*

After all, when was the last time you heard a werewolf—laugh?

With a sinking feeling in her stomach, Jessica hurried toward the noise. There in the corner of the hallway, near the stairs, crouched four boys—Brian, Charlie, Bruce Patman, and Aaron Dallas. They were laughing so hysterically they couldn't even speak.

"All right, you guys," Jessica demanded, "what's the big idea?"

Bruce and Brian gave each other high fives. Charlie was literally rolling around on the floor in glee. "We—we—" Aaron stuttered, his body wracked with giggles.

"Get up and tell us what's going on," Jessica ordered, her face turning red.

Aaron pointed to Charlie. Charlie held up his hand. It was covered with a long brown sock. Jessica's heart sank. She had a feeling that she and the other girls had made fools of themselves.

"And here's your broken glass, Jessica," Charlie added, holding up a tape player. When he hit the "play" button, Jessica heard the sound of glass being broken. "You sure were brave, Jess!" he gasped, doubling up with laughter.

"Oh, there's no way any dumb story can scare *you*," Aaron added, clutching his stomach. "No such thing as vampires, huh?"

Jessica put her hands on her hips. Taking a deep breath, she racked her brain for the most devastating comment she could make. She couldn't think of a single one.

Instead, Jessica narrowed her eyes in as sophisticated a way as she could manage. Holding her head high, she walked down the stairs, slowly at first, then faster and faster. She could hear the other girls following. Jessica felt her pulse. Her heart was still racing.

On the first floor, Jessica whirled to face her friends. "Something," she said furiously, "will have to be done about those boys."

Three

"The word is 'revenge,'" Jessica said that evening as she watched Elizabeth set the kitchen table. "Think, Lizzie. How are we going to get revenge on those boys?"

Elizabeth frowned as she set down a place mat. "I wish I knew."

"We can't let them get away with this," Jessica said warningly. "It's going to be all around school tomorrow, the way they embarrassed us. You might as well put it in the *Sweet Valley Sixers*, Lizzie. Write up a big headline. 'Bathroom Scare: Six Girls Terrified By Idiotic Boys.'"

At that moment, Steven came bounding in, home from basketball practice. "Hey!" he exclaimed happily when he saw the girls. "It's my sisters, the celebrities! Broken any glass lately?"

"Steven!" Elizabeth exclaimed.

"See what I mean?" Jessica said bitterly. "Even the high school kids know. We're going to have to move to Timbuktu, or somewhere."

"How about Transylvania?" Steven teased them. "I hear you can get a lot of great vampire tapes there. Just shove them into your tape player and scare the living daylights out of your friends."

"Steven, cut it out," Jessica told him.

"Hey, I've got a riddle for you," Steven continued, taking no notice of his sister. "What has twelve legs and screams?" He paused. "Six girls in the bathroom. Like it?"

"No," Jessica said.

"OK," Steven agreed. "Here's another. How can you tell which is Dracula and which is Charlie Cashman?"

"Dracula is better looking," Jessica said sullenly.

"You're supposed to say, 'I don't know,'" Steven said. "Then I say, 'Well, of course not. You can't tell; you're a sixth-grade girl.' Ha, ha, ha!" He slapped his knee with his palm.

"Very funny," Jessica said. "Now move, you're in my way. I think I'm going to help my sister set the table." She elbowed Steven as she went to the silverware drawer. Yanking it open, she pulled out a sharp knife. "I don't know whether to use this on you, or on those stupid boys," she muttered, pointing it at Steven.

"Revenge would be awfully sweet," Elizabeth

said, looking meaningfully at her twin.

Mr. Wakefield walked into the kitchen. "What's this about revenge?" he asked, eyeing the knife in Jessica's hand. Reluctantly, she lowered it.

"A bunch of boys scared us this afternoon, Dad, that's all," Jessica explained. "Elizabeth and I are figuring out how to get them back."

"I see," Mr. Wakefield said. "It looked to me like you were plotting some kind of revenge on Steven." He patted his son on the shoulder. "I know he's annoying, but we'd kind of like to keep him."

"I was innocent, Dad!" Steven said.

Mr. Wakefield only smiled. "I'm sure you were. Now how about using the knife to slice up some vegetables for dinner, Steven?"

"That was why I was handing it to him," Jessica said, putting on her most angelic voice. She got out the rest of the knives and began laying them around the table. "But I'll let him get out the vegetables himself."

Steven piled some cucumbers and carrots onto the cutting board. Elizabeth reached across him for a can of spaghetti sauce. "What kind of revenge are you planning?" Mr. Wakefield asked.

Jessica shrugged. "We don't know yet."

Mr. Wakefield opened a bottle of pop. "Well, let me know if you need any help," he said. "I used to be pretty good at scaring people, myself."

"You?" Steven asked.

"Uh-huh, me," Mr. Wakefield replied with a smile. "I bet I could give you some pointers."

Elizabeth opened the spaghetti sauce and set it next to the cutting board. "No, thanks, Dad," she said politely but firmly.

"No offense, Dad," Jessica added, "but we see special effects all the time. We need more than that to frighten us."

"Like a tape recording of broken glass?" Steven asked.

"That was different," Jessica argued, shooting her brother a dirty look. "Kids today don't need *Frankenstein*, or Poe." She carefully avoided saying *Dracula*. "We need something like Jason, or Freddy Kruger, instead."

"Freddy who?" Mr. Wakefield asked.

Jessica sighed. "Exactly."

"Jessica's right," Steven said from the kitchen counter.

Jessica looked at him in surprise. *Steven's defending me?* she asked herself.

"Monsters just won't cut it anymore," Steven continued. Waving his chopping knife in the air, he slammed it onto the cutting board. Suddenly his eyes bulged. "Aaaaah!" he screamed, a note of panic in his voice.

"What's wrong?" Jessica stood stock-still.

"Ow . . . ow . . . ow!" Steven screamed. "My finger—I think I cut it off!"

Jessica's mouth dropped open. "What were you

swinging that knife around for?" she shrieked.

Mr. Wakefield jumped up from his chair and rushed toward his son. Steven held up his hand.

Jessica gasped. There were only three fingers and a thumb, and red stuff was dripping from where the other finger should have been!

"Steven!" Mr. Wakefield exclaimed, grabbing a dish towel. "Call 911!" he urged Elizabeth. But Elizabeth was already on her way to the phone.

"We have to find the finger," Jessica said desperately. "I think they can sew it back on if we find it right away. Is it on the floor, Steven?" She ran to his side and began looking on the countertop. There was the knife. Jessica winced and started to turn away. . . .

Wait a minute.

That red stuff all over the knife looked familiar, all right, but Jessica knew for certain that it wasn't blood.

All at once Steven stopped wiggling and let go of his hand. Out popped the "missing" finger, covered with something that Jessica now recognized: spaghetti sauce. "Gotcha!" Steven crowed.

Spaghetti sauce. Jessica sank into the nearest chair. "Pretty lame, Steven," she said automatically, but she could feel her heart beating with a fury. *What a terrible trick.*

Steven hooted. "Admit it, Jess. Scarier than my face—and maybe even scarier than Frankenstein." He flexed his finger and ran the faucet to clean it off.

"The look on your face! Awesome!" He laughed.

Mr. Wakefield shook his head and managed a pale grin. "You really had us going for a minute, Steven," he said, wiping his forehead. "You might want to cool it with jokes like that, though, OK?"

"OK," Steven agreed cheerfully. He waltzed through the kitchen. "'Nothing is going to scare me,'" he said, quoting Jessica. "'Not for the next two weeks.' Ho, ho, ho."

"Drop dead, Steven," Jessica told him as she stood up. She kicked a piece of loose tile on the floor. First the scare in the bathroom, and now this. Things were not going well.

But as she walked into the dining room, Jessica realized that Steven had just given her an idea.

On Thursday afternoon, Jessica came into Mr. Bowman's class with a smile. Instead of sitting in the back row as usual, though, she headed for the front. "Hi, Charlie," she said, sliding into the seat next to him.

Charlie's head snapped up from the papers in front of him. "Huh?" he said. "Oh. Hi, Jessica." A grin began to play at the corners of his mouth. "Gee, I haven't seen you all day," he said. "Been up to the third floor again today? Just in case there are any vampires up there—yuk, yuk, yuk?" He elbowed Jessica in the ribs as he laughed.

Jessica felt like smacking him, but instead she flashed him her prettiest smile. "No, I haven't,

Charlie," she told him sweetly. "Have you?"

Charlie stopped laughing and shook his head. "No. Hey, what are you doing sitting up here, anyway?"

Jessica looked directly into Charlie's eyes. "I just thought I'd like to spend a little more time with you, that's all." *Yuck.* Jessica was glad she was a good actress.

"Oh." Charlie began to edge in the other direction. Turning around, he saw Lila in the chair on the other side from Jessica. "Where's Brian?" he asked, confused.

Jessica leaned even closer to him. "Lila got there first today," she whispered. "She and I wanted you all to ourselves."

Charlie looked from one girl to the other. Jessica was pleased to see that he was frowning. "I'm not going to sit next to you," he said rudely, collecting his books and struggling to his feet.

"What's the matter?" Jessica asked innocently. "You're not scared of us, are you? A big, strong boy like you?" Jessica was very proud of that line. She had practiced it several times last night in front of the mirror.

"Afraid of you? No way, Jose," Charlie said contemptuously. He started to thrust his chair back.

"Plan B," Jessica hissed to the row behind her.

Quickly, Elizabeth shoved her desk forward. The front of it slammed up against the back of Charlie's chair, neatly trapping him between Elizabeth's desk and his own.

"Hey!" Charlie glared back at Elizabeth. Elizabeth pretended not to notice. She was frantically looking through her notebook.

"I'm afraid she's busy, Charlie," Jessica pointed out, suppressing a giggle. "And class is really about to begin."

Charlie looked around worriedly. Then, shoving his own desk forward, he broke Jessica's grasp on his sweater and began to stand up.

"Oh, Charlie!" Jessica said with mock dismay.

"Hi, Jessica," Maria said calmly, stepping forward right on schedule and pushing Charlie's desk back at him. She leaned on its edge. "Hi, Charlie," she added in a throaty, movie star voice.

"Hi, Maria," Charlie grumbled, looking around frantically. Jessica bit her lip to keep from laughing.

When Mr. Bowman called the class to order, Maria returned to her seat. Mr. Bowman turned off the lights, as usual, but this time he lit a single candle and placed it on his desk. "So romantic, don't you think?" Jessica cooed in Charlie's ear. Charlie grimaced and slid toward Lila.

"Today's story," Mr. Bowman announced, "is by Robert Louis Stevenson, who also wrote *Treasure Island*. This one's about a scientist who invents a potion that changes his personality. Anyone know the name?"

Elizabeth raised her hand. "*Dr. Jekyll and Mr. Hyde*?" she asked.

Mr. Bowman grinned and nodded. Flipping

open the book, he began to read.

Jessica was pleased to see that Charlie was drawn into the story right away. When Mr. Bowman described how the mild-mannered Dr. Jekyll turned into the evil Mr. Hyde, Jessica watched closely as Charlie sat up straighter and fiddled nervously with his pencil. She looked across at Lila. "Ten minutes," she mouthed.

Lila gave the thumbs-up sign.

"Want some candy?" Jessica whispered to Charlie ten minutes later, rustling the box to attract his attention.

Charlie didn't take his eyes off Mr. Bowman. Jessica grinned. She thought his face looked downright pale. *He didn't even hear me,* she told herself with satisfaction.

"Psst! Charlie!" Jessica leaned a little more to her left. "Candy?"

"What?" Charlie asked distractedly.

"Candy," Jessica repeated. "It's free. Help yourself."

"Oh—OK." Charlie glanced at the box and then back at Mr. Bowman. On the other side, Jessica could see Lila watching the scene intently. Still looking at Mr. Bowman, Charlie reached in the box—and screamed.

The noise tore through the classroom like a gunshot. Alarmed, Mr. Bowman set down the book and jumped off his perch. A few students in the back of the room gasped. Even Jessica was startled, and she had been expecting something like this.

"Charlie, what on earth?" Mr. Bowman began.

"A finger, it's a dead finger!" Charlie yelled hysterically, jumping up out of his seat. He took a look into Jessica's box. "She did it!" he exclaimed, sobbing. "She showed me a box with a finger inside and told me it was candy! Then the finger moved!" Breathing hard, Charlie dashed forward to the front of the room. "Mr. Bowman, you've got to do something, it's awful, it's . . ."

"Oh, Charlie," Jessica interrupted with a loud sigh. "Must you be such a baby?" She looked around the room. Maria and Elizabeth were trying their best to hide their giggles, but Amy and Lila were already laughing out loud at the sight of Charlie pressed up against the chalkboard.

"Jessica," Mr. Bowman said firmly. "Suppose you tell us what the story is."

"Uh—*Dr. Jekyll and Mr. Hyde*?" Jessica ventured.

Mr. Bowman crossed his arms. "You know what I mean."

Jessica stood up. "He just opened the box," she said. "That's all."

"Show us what was inside," Mr. Bowman directed.

Jessica tilted the box forward and showed the class what looked like a finger. Only it was a terrible greenish-blackish color, as though it had been decomposing for several days. In places it was streaked with a red that looked like dried blood. Some of her classmates gasped. "It's a finger, all right," she said carelessly, "but it's not dead. It's mine." She showed the group how she had cut a little hole in the bottom of the box and stuck her finger through.

"And then you painted your finger?" Mr. Bowman asked.

"Yup," Jessica said, feeling happier than she'd felt in a couple of days. Charlie had stopped crying, but he was still shaking like a leaf. She pulled her finger out of the box and showed it off. "Pretty gross, huh?"

"Uh-huh," Mr. Bowman said dryly. "Jessica, I think you and I had better have a little talk."

"Oh, sure, Mr. Bowman," Jessica said. Not even being punished could dampen her spirits just now. Handing the box to Lila, she took one more satisfied look at Charlie and addressed the rest of the class.

"Boys are just so brave, aren't they?" she said with a smirk.

Four

Elizabeth arrived at school a little early on Friday morning. As she headed for her locker, she smiled, remembering Jessica's joke the day before. *I bet we won't be hearing from those boys again,* she told herself with satisfaction.

She began to spin the combination lock left to 36—and stopped. *Wait a minute.*

The locker wasn't fully closed. Had she left it open yesterday afternoon? Elizabeth reached for the handle, pulled open her locker—and gasped.

A Barbie doll, its head practically wrenched off, hung from the coat hook by a shoelace. Red stuff covered the doll. *Just ketchup,* Elizabeth told herself. But her heart beat wildly as she closed the door to the locker.

Elizabeth looked down the hallway. "Maria!"

she called to her friend, who was walking quickly toward their homeroom. "Come see this!" She opened the locker again so Maria could take a look.

"Ugh," Maria agreed, wrinkling her nose in disgust. "That's gross."

"It's only ketchup, isn't it?" Elizabeth asked, a note of concern creeping into her voice.

"It's only ketchup," Maria told her. "Just somebody's idea of a joke."

"Those stupid boys think they're so hysterical." Elizabeth stared at the doll. She knew she ought to take it off the hook, but she was reluctant to touch it. Ketchup or not, that red stuff certainly looked awfully real. She moved back a step. "Why don't you hand it to me, Maria," she suggested, "and I'll go put it in the garbage can."

Maria didn't budge. "I've got a better idea," she said. "It's your locker. Why don't you pick it up and give it to me to throw away?"

Elizabeth frowned. "Those boys are probably watching us right now," she told her friend. "They're probably laughing up a storm somewhere down the hall because we're afraid to touch a doll that someone dipped in ketchup."

"You're probably right," Maria said, making no move toward the Barbie.

Oh, honestly. Elizabeth stepped forward. Clenching her teeth firmly, she undid the shoelace from the hook. She pulled the Barbie out, still holding it by the string. Up close, she decided, it was even more obvious that the "blood" was only ketchup. Elizabeth reached out to touch it—

Then she drew her hand back.

"Even more obvious" still wasn't a hundred percent.

"What's this?" Maria bent down and picked up a piece of paper that had blown out of Elizabeth's locker.

"I don't know," Elizabeth told her as she walked to the garbage can and, with relief, dropped the Barbie in. "I usually keep my papers inside my school binder."

"Wait just a minute here!" Maria's voice was excited.

"What is it?" Elizabeth asked.

"Look at this." Grimly, Maria held out the paper for Elizabeth to read. Scrawled in red crayon were the words THE SCARE WAR IS ON!

"Mystery meat today," Jessica sighed later on that afternoon. She was sitting with some of the other Unicorns at the Unicorner, their usual table in the school cafeteria.

"Mystery meat and mystery vegetables," Mandy Miller agreed. She picked up something that looked a little like a pea and a little like a lima bean. "Do you think that this would bounce if I dropped it?"

Jessica pretended to consider the question. "It'd probably break the floor."

"Probably," Lila said with a smile. She pushed all

the vegetables over to the side of her plate. "You know, the strangest thing happened to me this morning."

Jessica pricked up her ears. Next to her, Mary Wallace and Ellen Riteman stopped their conversation, too. "What was it?" Jessica asked.

"I left my bookbag in the hall for a few minutes," Lila explained, "and when I came back, there was a huge red sign on it that said 'DON'T SCARE US—WE'LL SCARE YOU.'"

"Really?" Jessica thought she knew who might be responsible for that one. "Pretty lame, if you ask me."

Lila laughed. "Well—yes," she said, stabbing a piece of meat with her fork. "Of course, the ketchup spots made it a little scarier. At first, I mean," she added quickly. "Once I realized it was only ketchup, I wasn't worried about it at all."

"Oh." Jessica took a sip of milk. "So you weren't really scared."

"Of course not!" Lila looked shocked. "I mean, it was only ketchup."

"How did you know?" Mandy asked. "Did you taste it?"

Lila gave Mandy an exasperated look. "I can tell the difference between ketchup and blood without having to taste it, you know."

Before Jessica could ask her anything more Janet arrived at the table and put down her tray with a bang. "Jessica," she said sharply as she sat down. Jessica's heart sank. "I don't like to point fingers,"

Janet continued. "I'm not the kind of person who goes around blaming others—am I, girls?" Ellen, Mary, Lila, and Mandy nodded in agreement that Janet certainly did not go around blaming others.

"But if anyone's responsible for this, it's you," Janet said, looking straight at Jessica and narrowing her eyes.

Jessica looked back and swallowed. "I'm sorry, Janet," she said hastily. Jessica had learned long ago that apologizing to Janet was often a good idea—even if you hadn't done anything wrong. "Um—what am I apologizing for?" she asked.

Janet picked up a folded piece of purple construction paper.

"I don't have anything to do with that. I've never even seen it before," Jessica pointed out.

Janet sighed. "I never said you did, Jessica. Look at it closely. What do you notice?"

Jessica strained her eyes. "Well, it's kind of squarish," she ventured.

Janet made a snorting noise in her throat.

Wrong answer. Jessica licked her lips nervously. "Uh—it's purple," she tried again.

"Uh-huh." Janet nodded with satisfaction. "And what is important about the color purple?"

Jessica was delighted to get such an easy question. "Purple is the official Unicorn color," she said automatically. All club members were required to wear something purple to school each day. "If that's what you're worrying about, my pants are purple today. See?" Jessica stood up.

"Don't bother, Jessica." Janet nodded meaningfully. "I don't know about you girls," she said, turning to the rest of the table, "but I'm president of the Unicorn Club. When I find a piece of purple paper in my locker, I expect it to be official Unicorn correspondence."

What in the world? Jessica wondered. *Official Unicorn correspondence? We hardly ever write each other letters.* She looked around the table. The other girls were all nodding. Apparently they also expected all their purple papers to be official Unicorn Club stationery.

"And I certainly didn't expect this!" With a sudden motion, Janet seized the paper, opened it up, and thrust it into Jessica's face.

Jessica instinctively moved back. As her eyes came into focus, she gasped. There was blood all over the paper—

Or wait a minute, a little voice in her head told her. *That's not blood, that's just ketchup.*

"That's ketchup," Jessica stammered when she found her voice.

Janet sighed and rolled her eyes. "Naturally," she said, sounding bored. "Even a fourth grader would know that. I could tell right away."

"How?" Jessica asked. "Did you taste it?"

"Certainly not!" Janet sniffed. "And I didn't start screaming about blood so the entire school could hear—unlike some people I could mention." Janet stared hard at Lila.

Lila turned bright red. Jessica couldn't help smiling.

Janet snapped the paper in front of Jessica again. "But read what it says," she commanded.

"REVENGE," Jessica read.

"Exactly." Janet folded the paper up neatly and put it into her purse.

Jessica noticed she took care not to touch any of the ketchup stains. "But I still don't understand," she began. "What does this have to do with me?"

Janet rolled her eyes. "Who was responsible for getting these boys to go after us?" She tapped her fingers on the table and leaned forward.

Jessica was confused. "You mean my trick yesterday?"

"No," Janet barked. "Who was it who made me come along to the bathroom with her on Tuesday? Only because she was scared? I won't tell you her name, but her initials are Jessica Wakefield."

"What?" Jessica couldn't believe what she was hearing. "We were all—" But she caught herself. *What good will it do to argue with Janet?* she thought. *None.* Sometimes it was hard work being a Unicorn. "I'm sorry, Janet," she said softly. "I really am."

"That's better," Janet said. She sounded a little happier. Jessica sighed with relief. "Those boys need to be taught a lesson," Janet went on. "I suggest we meet at Jessica's house after school. All in favor?"

The vote was unanimous.

*   *   *

"I love weekends," Amy Sutton said after school that day.

"Two whole days off," Maria agreed, "and you don't even have to do homework till Sunday night."

"If you can get away with it," Elizabeth corrected. The three friends were cooking brownies in the Wakefield kitchen. "My scary book for English class is pretty long," she said. "I'm going to have to start tonight."

Maria smiled. "You'll like reading it," she predicted. "And then it isn't really homework, is it?"

"You're right," Elizabeth said with a grin. She thrust the tray into the oven. "In fact, this afternoon would be totally perfect," she said, "except for two things."

"Which are?" Amy asked.

"Number one," Elizabeth told them, ticking it off on her finger. "The Snob Squad is here."

"Don't remind me," Amy sighed.

"What's the second reason?" Maria asked.

"Those boys," Elizabeth said.

"Hmm," Maria said slowly. "You know, I heard that some of the Unicorns had practical jokes played on them today, too. Someone told me that Janet Howell practically had heart failure when Charlie shoved a letter into her locker."

"Wow!" Amy exclaimed. "You have to admit, it takes some guts to cross Queen Janet."

Elizabeth smiled. "You're right. And there's no way she'd let them get away with it. In fact, they're probably up there right now, plotting revenge."

A door opened upstairs. Jessica came down the steps and into the kitchen. "Mmm, brownies," she said. "Can I help you lick the bowl?"

"Just a taste," Elizabeth said, passing her the wooden stirring spoon. Usually she didn't care what the Unicorns were up to, but the scare war challenge had made her curious. "What are you talking about up there, anyway, Jess?" she asked.

Jessica fixed her sister with a look. "You know I can't tell you about club business, Lizzie. It's priveleged Unicorn information."

"The privileged Unicorn information wouldn't have anything to do with a scare war, would it?" Elizabeth asked.

"Well—" Jessica sighed and put her hands on her hips.

"Because, actually," Maria began, her eyes lighting up, "it might be a good idea for all of us to join forces against the guys. More power in numbers and all that."

Jessica folded her arms. "No offense or anything," she said, "but you don't exactly have the right kind of ideas where guys are concerned."

I do so, Elizabeth thought angrily, but she didn't say it. Instead she shrugged. "Have it your way," she said. "Too bad you'll never find out about the frozen red Jell-O trick."

"The what?" Jessica asked, a frown crossing her face.

"The what?" Amy repeated.

Elizabeth shot Amy a look. "Oh, nothing much," she said. "Just an idea we had for scaring the daylights out of some of those boys. But since you're not interested, we'll have to do it alone."

"The frozen red Jell-O trick?" Jessica asked slowly.

"Not to mention the fried cockroach prank," Maria added in a bored voice. "We've got a bunch of ideas."

"We do?" Amy asked.

Elizabeth stepped carefully on Amy's foot. "We've been talking about it for a while," she said. "But you Unicorns have plenty of imagination, too. Janet, Lila . . ." *Actually, I can't imagine anyone with less imagination than those two,* she told herself with a grin. "I guess you've made a list of everything you want to do, right?"

Jessica hesitated. "Do you guys really have lots of ideas?" she said.

"Tons of them," Elizabeth told her, crossing her fingers. *At least, we'll have tons of ideas once we think of them,* she said to herself.

Jessica seemed to make up her mind. "OK," she agreed. "As long as we can have some of your brownies."

"It's a deal," Elizabeth said.

"It seems to me that we have plenty of interesting suggestions about ways to scare the boys," Janet said a few minutes later. "Elizabeth, read some of them back."

She acts like she's president of the whole world, not just the Unicorns, Elizabeth thought with a sigh, but she did as she was told. The list was a long one. "So should we get started on Monday morning?" she asked when she had finished reading.

Janet frowned. "I think we should try some of them out first."

The girls looked at each other. "Try them on who?" Amy asked.

"We need a guinea pig," Janet explained. "A human guinea pig that we can test these scares out on."

"Oh, I see what you mean," Jessica said slowly. "The tricks that scare the guinea pig, we play on the boys next week."

"And the ones that don't work, we dump," Maria added. "It sounds OK to me. But where do we find a guinea pig?"

At that moment, a dreadful noise came floating up the stairs. "What on earth is that?" Janet asked, clamping her hands across her ears.

"That," Jessica sighed, "is our so-called brother."

"It's Johnny Buck tunes," Elizabeth put in. "He thinks he's singing Johnny's new song, 'Gotcha,' but he can't sing on key."

Jessica went to the top of the stairs. "Turn off the chain saw!" she shouted. "We're having a meeting up here!"

Steven only sang louder. *If you could call it singing,* Elizabeth thought, shaking her head.

"'Gonna getcha, gonna getcha . . .'" Mandy sang

along. She shook her head sadly. "Too bad. It's such a great song. 'Gonna getcha, gonna getcha.'"

"Gotcha!" Janet yelled, suddenly jumping up.

Elizabeth smothered a grin. The other girls stared. Janet didn't often lose her composure, even over Johnny Buck.

When she saw everyone staring at her, Janet cleared her throat. "What I mean is, Steven's the one," she said, her voice now calm. "Our guinea pig."

"Steven?" Elizabeth repeated.

A wolfish grin was forming on Janet's lips. "Jessica and Elizabeth, this is your job for the weekend. Try out all these pranks on him, and let us know what works for Monday."

"You're on!" Jessica said.

Elizabeth frowned. "Wait a second, Jess. That really doesn't sound very nice. After all, he is our brother."

Janet snorted. "Nice? You're talking about nice?" She sighed and folded her arms. "I knew we shouldn't have let your sister in on this, Jessica. Little Miss Congeniality wouldn't even hurt a fly."

"I—" Elizabeth began.

"It's not like he's nice to us," Jessica said quickly, turning to her sister. "I mean, listen to the way he sings off key. And some of those jokes he made about us? And—"

"I know, I know," Elizabeth cut in. "It's just that he didn't start the Scare War, and I don't think it's right to involve him—that's all."

"Come on, Lizzie," Jessica began. Elizabeth could hear her brother come stomping up the stairs, still singing loudly. "I mean, listen to him. He's only doing it to bother us, you know."

"Well, yes, but—"

Steven poked his head in the door. "Having a party and you didn't invite me?" he asked, pretending to be horrified.

"Steven, get out of here," Jessica ordered.

Steven retreated so the tips of his shoes were just outside the door. "Like this?" he asked, flashing them a huge grin. "Hey, I know why this room is so full. It's like the old joke. You ever hear the old joke?"

"Go away!" Jessica demanded, starting to get up.

"Then I'll tell it to you," Steven announced. "What's the difference between a pig and a middle-school girl?" When no one said anything, he answered himself: "The pig can go to the bathroom all by itself. Yuk, yuk, yuk!" He slammed the door shut and ran off downstairs.

"The nerve," Ellen whispered.

"Do you see what I mean, Lizzie?" Jessica began, eyes blazing. "He's obviously—"

"Save your breath, Jessica," Elizabeth interrupted her twin. She couldn't remember the last time she'd felt so humiliated. "I'm with you!"

Before bed that night, Elizabeth began to read *The Hound of the Baskervilles*. The story told of a murderous wild dog that haunted the plains of

England. The dog's footprints had been found near a dead body. No one knew whether the hound was real—or a ghost. The first few chapters were awfully good, she had to admit. And a little spooky, too. At last, with a yawn, she put the book aside and turned off the light.

But Elizabeth had trouble falling asleep. Her thoughts seemed to keep coming back to the ghostly hound. She tried to think about school. The next moment, though, she found herself thinking about huge wild dogs. She forced herself to concentrate on the tricks they were going to play on Steven the next day. But all at once, she was imagining the spooky, treeless plains of England.

Finally, Elizabeth did manage to fall asleep, but in the middle of the night, she woke up suddenly. She could feel her heart racing. The house seemed dark and frightening. *What was that noise?*

Forcing herself to lie still and breathe slowly, Elizabeth listened hard. *Arf. Arf, arf.* The hound! With a gasp, Elizabeth sat up—and realized she was safely in her own room. There wasn't any hound; it was just the neighbor's dog. Laughing a little at herself, she got up and turned on the light in the hallway. Then she climbed back into bed, leaving her bedroom door wide open.

It's not that I'm scared or anything, she told herself. *It's—just in case.*

Five

Steven woke up early on Saturday and looked up at the ceiling. *I love Saturday mornings*, he thought happily. No school, no chores, too early on the weekend to start worrying about homework. Plenty of time for swimming, bike riding, basketball—and, of course, tormenting sisters.

He could hardly wait.

Steven propped himself up on his pillows and yawned. *Let's see*, he told himself, *I should be able to come up with another good joke to tease them. Knock, knock*, he thought, and answered out loud, "Who's there?"

Hmm. How about a tape recorder? "A tape recorder," he said. *Aha.* "A tape recorder? Aaaaah!" he said softly, and chuckled. Of course, he'd have to get together with a friend to do it properly. His friend would say "Knock, knock," then Steven would say "Who's there?," his friend would say "A tape recorder," and Steven would scream the loudest scream ever, "Aaaaah!" Perfect. Steven stretched contentedly.

What was that?

It felt as if his toe had hit something. Curious, Steven stretched his foot out again. Yup, there was something down at the bottom of his bed, all right. Something hard . . . something—something *that moved when you touched it.*

Steven jerked his foot away. Then he decided he'd better get up altogether. Standing next to the bed, he reached out gently and touched the bedspread where the thing had been. Whatever it was, it was long and thin—and it still moved when you touched it.

Holding his breath, Steven jerked the bedspread away. Maybe it was only a bunched-up place in the sheet. Or an old belt. Or, better yet, maybe it was all his imaginati—

"AAAAAH!"

Steven leaped in the air and dashed out of the room, still yelling. "Mom! Dad!" he cried, barely able to get the words out. "There's—there's a—" He couldn't seem to say the rest. His voice sounded thick, not like his at all, and his chin felt like a block of wood. "Help!" he managed to yell.

Doors banged. Mr. Wakefield came running out of his room and put his hand on Steven's arm. "Are you hurt?" he asked.

"Not hurt," Steven gasped. "In there—" He pointed toward his bedroom. "It's a snake," he blurted out, trying to calm himself long enough to tell the story. "A snake, and it's big and long and—" He gulped for air. "And it was all coiled and ready to strike," he finished.

"A snake?" Mr. Wakefield pulled his robe closer around his shoulders.

Jessica came out of her room, looking very wide awake for so early in the morning. "A snake?" she gasped, shrinking back and opening her eyes wide. She leaned against the wall, fanning herself

Elizabeth helped to prop her twin against the wall. "Is it poisonous?" she asked Steven, arching her eyebrows.

"Probably," Steven told her, trying to remember exactly what it looked like. Fortunately, he hadn't seen it for long. "It was huge," he continued, "and its teeth were about three inches long, and I think it rattled at me—"

Steven broke off, frowning. It seemed as though Elizabeth was grinning. "Well, it did!" he insisted angrily.

"Of course it did, Steven," Elizabeth assured him. "I understand why you're so afraid. Those big black ones are the worst."

"They sure are," Steven agreed, nodding vigorously. "They—" He broke off once again and peered at his sister. "What do you mean, black? How did you know what color it was?"

"Well—" Elizabeth blushed. "I mean—that is—"

Steven narrowed his eyes. "I see." The realization began to sink in: He'd been tricked. He turned to his father and put on as sharp and dignified a voice as he could manage. "Well, never mind, Dad. I'll take care of this one myself. Thanks anyway." He closed his door before anyone could say another word.

The snake was still sitting coiled on the bed. Steven could see now that it didn't have teeth three inches long; in fact, the whole snake probably wouldn't stretch two feet if you unwound it.

He picked it up carefully by the tail and dumped it in the trash can. *It sure looks real*, he grumbled. Just to be on the safe side, he dropped a few old pieces of newspaper on top.

"We're really sorry, Steven," Jessica said earnestly at breakfast.

"Really," Elizabeth chimed in.

Jessica tried to hide a grin. "We just couldn't resist, that's all. No hard feelings, huh?"

"All right," Steven said grudgingly.

"And no more pranks. We promise." Jessica crossed her fingers behind her back. "Here. Let me fix you some cereal. Cap'n Crunch, right?"

Steven nodded. Jessica got out the cereal and the milk. "You like to have a lot, don't you, Steven?" she asked conversationally as she poured the cereal in the bowl. "I'll fill it to the brim." She poured in some milk. *Hmm.* As the milk filled up the bowl, a plastic spider popped up from under the cereal and floated to the top.

"One bowl of Cap'n Crunch coming up!" Jessica announced. Carefully she carried it to the table and set the bowl in front of Steven. Then she stood back and watched.

Steven set down the sports page and looked at the bowl. His eyes widened, and he snapped his head around to stare accusingly at Jessica.

"Oh, come *on*," he said, rolling his eyes.

Oh, well, Jessica thought. She forced an apologetic smile onto her face.

"Sorry," she said, shrugging her shoulders. "We shouldn't have tried to fool an old pro like you with a stupid trick like this."

"It was stupid, all right," Steven agreed importantly.

"Yeah," Jessica said. She hung her head. "Well, we won't do it again. Elizabeth, why don't you get another bowl for Steven?"

"I mean, plastic spiders." Steven sniffed when the new bowl arrived. "What do you think I am, anyway? Dumb or something?" He grabbed his spoon and started taking huge mouthfuls.

"Oh, no, you're certainly not dumb," Jessica told him, trying to suppress a smile.

"When you've been around as long as I have," Steven said, chewing a bite and waving his spoon around for emphasis, "you start to learn what tricks will work and which ones won't. See, that one with the spider didn't work because of the element of surprise."

"Element of surprise," Elizabeth agreed, pretending to write it down.

"Uh-huh, surprise." Steven swallowed and loaded his spoon up again. "I mean, I knew you were planning something."

"You did?" Jessica stared closely at Steven's bowl.

"It was obvious." Steven swallowed again and forced his spoon back into the cereal bowl. "I let you have your fun," he explained, taking yet another bite. "But I was prepared for anything. You could have dropped a nuclear bomb on me and I would have been ready—" Suddenly Steven grimaced and coughed. He stuck his tongue far out of his mouth and made a gagging sound.

"Something wrong, Steven?" Jessica asked sweetly.

Steven held up something large that he'd pulled off his tongue. It was only about an inch long, but it was so covered with milk and cereal that it was hard to tell what it was. Steven yelled and thrust his bowl violently in the opposite direction. Milky mush spilled out all over the table. Frantically Steven wiped away the cereal on the object that had been in his mouth.

"Aaaaah!" he screamed for the second time that day.

"Make a note of it," Jessica told her sister as they stood by the sink. "Rubber cockroaches are ten times better than plastic spiders."

"Got it," Elizabeth agreed.

"Steven?" Mrs. Wakefield appeared in the doorway. She looked tired. "What on earth are you up to now?"

"I'm going out to the pool," Steven snapped after lunch that day. "No more pranks!"

Mrs. Wakefield looked gravely at the twins. "Are you listening to what your brother says, girls?"

"Yes, Mom," Elizabeth said quietly.

"It's not that they're frightening me or anything," Steven explained to his mother. "It's just annoying, that's all. Hey, I could come up with better tricks than these with both eyes shut." He stood up, grabbed a towel, and headed off for the backyard.

Elizabeth stood up quickly. "If you'll excuse us, Mom," she said, "Jessica and I have something to do. We're in the middle of an important experiment."

Mrs. Wakefield folded her arms. "For school, you mean?"

"Yes," Jessica said loudly just as Elizabeth said, "You could say that."

Elizabeth cleared her throat. "Anyway, can we be excused, please? To do this thing for school."

"All right." Mrs. Wakefield sighed. "Just don't do anything too drastic, all right? I know Steven can be annoying, but I really can't allow you to do anything too awful to him."

"I can't imagine why," Jessica told Elizabeth as soon as they were out of earshot.

"Me neither." Elizabeth pulled out her notebook. "'Frozen red Jell-O,'" she read, delighted that she'd thought of a trick using it. "'Wrap it in a tissue and put it next to someone's skin.' We've got plenty of skin to choose from," she said, staring over at her brother. He was lying on a deck chair near the pool, wearing only a swimsuit.

"He's singing again," Jessica remarked with distaste. "Now, who's got better aim, you or me?"

Elizabeth hefted the package of Jell-O they'd mixed the night before and frozen. "I think I can do this one," she told her sister.

"All right." Jessica nodded. "We can get pretty close, anyway. Aim for the chest. He can't hear a thing because of the music, and he's got his eyes closed."

Elizabeth took several steps forward. Steven didn't move.

"Closer," Jessica whispered.

"We need to be able to escape," Elizabeth replied, edging nearer anyway. She handed Jessica the notebook. "You stay behind this bush and watch. I'll join you when I can."

Jessica nodded and took up her position.

Elizabeth took two more steps forward. She wrapped the tissue tighter and focused on Steven's bare chest.

"Come on!" Jessica hissed from behind the bush.

Suddenly Steven's chest seemed as large as a house to Elizabeth. How could she possibly miss? She let fly. The Jell-O came straight down in the middle of the target.

"Aaaaah!" For the third time that day Steven screamed. Elizabeth dashed behind the bush.

"It works very nicely," Elizabeth whispered to Jessica, as she watched Steven cowering underneath the deck chair. "Now would you say he jumped three feet in the air, or was it only two and a half?"

"It's almost too easy," Elizabeth complained a little later. Dropping peeled grapes down Steven's shirt had been a tremendous success.

"What do you mean?" Jessica flipped through Elizabeth's notebook.

"Well, look." Elizabeth pointed to the list. "On a scale of one to ten, almost everything's a ten." Jessica watched as her twin's finger moved down the column. "Everything except the spider, really. I just wonder if Steven's—well, typical." She shut the notebook.

Jessica waved her hand dismissively. "Of course he's typical," she scoffed. "Boys are all alike."

"Do you think so?" Elizabeth frowned.

"I *know* so." Jessica thought back to the finger trick she'd pulled in English class. Steven certainly hadn't been any more terrified than Charlie had been that afternoon. "And anyway, we're dealing with boys like Brian and Charlie here. They're not exactly big and strong and fearless, if you know what I mean."

"Uh-huh." Elizabeth nodded reluctantly.

"Look," Jessica continued, "it just tells us that these tricks are pretty darn good, that's all. He didn't fall for the spider, did he?" Elizabeth shook her head. "So it's not just any old trick that'll fool him. It has to be something *good*."

Elizabeth sighed. "OK. I guess you're right. What's next?"

Jessica opened the notebook again. "Let's see. Steven's swimming now, so—putting red food coloring in the showerhead."

"What if he doesn't take a shower after he swims today?" Elizabeth wanted to know.

Jessica sighed impatiently. "Steven always takes a shower after he swims. Don't you remember? He told us a couple of years ago that the chlorine peels off all your skin if you don't. Pretty silly." Jessica decided not to mention that she, herself, had always taken a shower after swimming ever since then.

"That's right," Elizabeth said. "OK, let's do it."

Quickly the girls unscrewed the outdoor shower-head. Jessica filled the nozzle with red food coloring and screwed it back on. They watched as Steven got out of the pool, picked up his towel, and headed for the shower. Jessica tried to channel messages toward Steven. *Get in and turn the water on,* she found herself saying over and over. She was afraid that Steven would turn the water on first instead.

Steven stepped into the shower area. Jessica held her breath as he pulled the knobs to ON.

A red waterfall cascaded over Steven's head and shoulders. Elizabeth grabbed Jessica's shoulder. "It isn't bothering him," she whispered.

Jessica didn't take her eyes off Steven. "He's got his eyes shut," she whispered back. "Just wait." She could see Steven turn around, open his eyes, and—

"On a scale of one to ten?" Jessica asked as the screams began.

Elizabeth grinned. "Nine and a half," she replied.

Jessica shook her head. "Ten," she corrected.

They listened as the screams continued, rising even higher in pitch. Jessica thought she could just make out the word "blood."

The girls looked at each other. "Eleven," they said together.

"How about when we sailed those helium balloons wrapped in white sheets into his room?" Jessica asked Sunday afternoon.

Elizabeth considered. "Nine and a half," she

said. "We probably should have painted glow-in-the-dark eyes on them."

"Did we buy glow-in-the-dark paint?" Jessica asked.

Elizabeth nodded. "Plastic spiders, helium balloons, glow-in-the-dark paints—you name it, we bought it. I bet we're broke by now."

"Probably," Jessica said. "Nine and a half, huh? I'd give the same rating to the tape-recorded screams we played in his closet last night."

"Why so low?" Elizabeth asked.

Jessica scratched her chin. "You had to hide in there, and that made it tricky. If we could have figured out some way to rig up a remote control, it might have been a perfect ten."

"Hmm. Good point." Elizabeth entered the scores into her notebook. "Only one trick left."

Jessica's eyes danced. "The big one."

Elizabeth grinned. "The timing's perfect. No one's home but us and Steven, and Maria said she'd be ready right about now. The only thing we have to wait for is for Steven to take a snack."

"That won't take long," Jessica commented. "Not the way he eats."

"Another good point," Elizabeth agreed, getting up from her seat. "You go into the kitchen. I'll wait out here."

"I just want a snack," Steven told Jessica as he bounded into the kitchen two minutes later. "Any chance I can have one without ghosts, goblins, ghoulies, or frozen Jell-O?"

"Help yourself," Jessica replied in a bored voice, barely looking up from her fashion magazine.

"How about a candy bar?" Steven continued. "Does this meet with your approval?" He reached into the pantry and held a candy bar up in the air.

"Yeah, whatever," Jessica answered, keeping her eyes glued to the page.

She listened as Steven tore open the wrapper and began chewing. *One, two, three,* Jessica counted to herself. Then she looked up and let out a scream. "Steven!" she cried, standing up.

"What's the matter?" Steven asked sarcastically. "Was this yours or something?" He took another bite.

Jessica began pulling on the hairs on her arms. She found that this was a good way to give herself a pale, panicked look. "Steven," she said shakily, "you—you didn't eat that, did you?"

Steven sighed loudly. "No, I'm not finished with it yet, sister dear, but I plan to be soon. Now if you'll leave me alone—"

"Steven," Jessica whispered, her face aghast, "don't you know what was in that candy bar?"

"Hmm, let's see," Steven said with a look of phony curiosity as he checked the label. "Chocolate. And some nuts." He looked back at Jessica. "And speaking of nuts—have you *totally* lost it?"

Jessica crossed the room and laid her hand on

Steven's sleeve. "Steven," she said, locking his eyes with her own, "that candy bar was the one Mom and Dad poisoned to feed to the rats in the basement!"

Steven snorted. "You think I'll believe that?" he asked. "You've been trying to fool me all weekend long, and I'm totally sick of it—"

"Steven, you have to believe me!" Jessica said imploringly. She was working so hard to look distressed, she was starting to give herself a headache. "There's poison in that candy!"

"Yeah, sure," Steven said, stepping back. He set down the rest of the candy on the counter. "Really scary, sis. I mean, I'm terrified."

"Lizzie!" Jessica burst out. "Lizzie, come quick!" She turned back to Steven, who seemed to be holding a bite of candy in his mouth instead of swallowing it. "Don't worry, Steven," she said with forced calm. "We'll take care of everything. We'll make sure you live."

"What's going on?" Elizabeth asked, dashing into the kitchen.

Jessica silently pointed to the candy wrapper.

"Oh, no," Elizabeth whispered. She covered her mouth with her hands. "Steven. Oh, you didn't."

"I think our only chance is to get him to the hospital right away," Jessica continued frantically, stumbling over her words. "Maybe they can, I don't know, pump out his stomach or something."

She waved her hands in the air and took a deep breath.

"But Mom and Dad are at a party," Elizabeth protested. She looked at Steven with a note of doom in her voice. She was delighted to see that he looked slightly pale. "I guess we have no other choice: he'll have to ride his bike there."

"Cut it out, you guys!" Steven protested, turning still a little paler. "There's no rat poison in that candy bar."

Jessica grabbed Steven by the arm and started to steer him toward the door. "Hurry!" she said. Steven took a couple of steps, but then he stopped short. "This is ridiculous!" he told her.

Jessica stared at Elizabeth. "He doesn't have much time left!" she wailed. "What'll we do?"

"I know!" Elizabeth said as if a bright idea had just occurred to her. "Let's call Mom. She'll let him know."

"That's a great idea!" Jessica burst out. "Where's the number?"

Elizabeth rummaged through a pile of papers till she found what she was looking for. "I'll dial for you, Steven," she said, punching numbers in. "Then you can talk— Hello?" she said into the receiver. "May I speak to Mrs. Wakefield, please?"

Maria Slater answered. "Is that you, Elizabeth?"

"I'll wait," Elizabeth said loudly.

Maria giggled. "OK, I'm ready. Let 'er rip!"

"Mom?" Elizabeth said quickly. "It's me. Listen,

Steven needs to talk to you." She held out the phone to her brother, who seemed to be looking worse by the minute.

"Mom?" he said weakly, taking the receiver from Elizabeth's grasp. "There isn't poison in the candy bar, is there?"

Leaning close, Elizabeth could overhear Maria's reaction. "In the candy bar?" she said in a voice that sounded exactly like Mrs. Wakefield's. Elizabeth grinned across at her sister. *Good thing we have a friend who's a professional actress*, she thought. Maria could imitate Mrs. Wakefield perfectly! "Oh, Steven—"

Steven gulped. "It is?" he asked.

"There's only one thing to do," Maria told him. "Are you strong enough to ride your bike?"

"Yeah, well, I—"

"Ride your bike down to the hospital and ask them to pump out your stomach," Maria continued. "Your father and I will be there in twenty minutes or so."

"But—" Steven began, a look of terror coming into his face.

"No buts," Maria told him. "Now go!" There was a click.

Steven looked at his sisters. "I gotta go," he said thickly. "Be seeing you—I hope!" He dashed out the door.

"Excellent," Jessica said approvingly. "The best one yet. Now—remind me. How far toward the hospital do we let him go?"

"He has to pass Maria's house," Elizabeth said with a smile. "She's there with Amy. They'll be waiting for him. She'll let him know."

Jessica's body shook with laughter. "In Mom's voice, of course."

"Of course," Elizabeth replied, trying to keep a straight face.

What a terrific weekend, Jessica thought on Sunday night. *And what a chicken we have for a brother!* She opened her book of short stories by Edgar Allan Poe and chose one called "The Black Cat." Jessica liked cats. Also, it looked short.

It isn't very scary, she told herself after a few pages. *There's no blood, no severed heads, no corpses walking at midnight—just this black cat that makes the narrator nervous. Pretty silly, if you ask me.*

As Jessica read on, she had to admit that the story was kind of, well, interesting. She also had to admit that it gave her the sense that something, well, unpleasant was about to happen. Something involving the black cat. Then, for no reason at all, she happened to look up.

Looking through the window was a very large, very black cat.

Jessica's body went numb. She stiffened. Then, slowly, she relaxed. *That's only Big Jim from down the street*, she told herself. *Nothing to be afraid of.* But Jessica put down her book anyway.

Six

◇

"How did the experiment go?" Lila asked at lunch on Monday. Jessica was sitting with some of the other Unicorns at the Unicorner.

"Excellent," Jessica replied. "Steven was a great guinea pig. You were right, Janet."

The leader of the Unicorns sniffed. "Let me see your list, Jessica."

Jessica handed her a copy. Janet flipped through it. "You mean everything worked?" she said at last.

"Uh-huh." Jessica nodded, barely able to keep the pride out of her voice. "That is, everything except the spider."

Janet glanced at Jessica. "Which tricks would you recommend we try, Jessica? Based on the results of your experiment, I mean."

Jessica realized with pleasure that all eyes were

on her. "Well," she began in an important-sounding voice, "the other tricks with bugs and snakes were really good. We just have to make sure they're made out of rubber, that's all. And the trick about the poison—we can do something with that one too, I think."

"How about the shower?" Janet demanded.

"It sounds like it worked," Lila said, taking a mouthful of spaghetti. "But I don't see how we can possibly do it here at school."

Janet shot Lila a furious look. Just in time, Jessica remembered that the shower trick had been Janet's idea. "It might have been the best trick of all, Lila," Jessica said honestly. "Maybe someone can sneak into the boys' locker room and do something to the showers. I was thinking we could keep that one in reserve—you know, as a way to get them for sure in case everything else doesn't work out."

"Excellent thinking," Janet said. "Exactly what I was going to say myself. Jessica, you've done a fine job."

Jessica felt her cheeks turning pink. Her lips curved upward into a smile. "Thank you, Janet," she said.

"So who wants to do what?" Mary Wallace asked. "What's the plan?"

To her delight, Jessica found that Ellen, Mandy, and Mary were looking straight at her instead of Janet. "Well," she began, and then she paused. She stole a quick glance at Janet, who was looking furious. Maybe trying to be the leader wasn't such a good idea after all. "I think Janet should decide that," Jessica finished.

Janet's face relaxed into a smile again. "Good thinking, Jessica."

Jessica was blushing more deeply when Elizabeth came by the table. "Did you tell them about the weekend, Jess? We really—"

"Aaaaah!" Lila suddenly gasped. She jerked her fork away from her tray as though she'd been bitten.

Jessica started out of her seat. "What's going on?" she began.

"It's a snail!" Lila cried, pointing to her food.

"Oh, my gosh!" Ellen shrieked.

Mandy abruptly stood up and moved back from the table.

But Jessica only shook her head. "It's just those boys again," she said loudly.

Elizabeth smiled. "A pretty lame trick if you ask me," she agreed. She reached down and picked up the snail off Lila's spaghetti. "Hmm, plastic." She sniffed. "Not exactly a high-class trick."

"According to our experiments, rubber is much more effective," Jessica added. She was pleased to see that the girls around the table had stopped drawing back from the snail and were now crowding around to see it better. "Were any of those boys anywhere near you in the cafeteria line?" Jessica demanded.

Lila nodded, still looking a little scared.

"Then that's what happened." Jessica shrugged. "But it's nothing to be afraid of. This is pretty poorly done, wouldn't you say, Elizabeth?"

"Oh, yes," Elizabeth agreed. "One thing we learned over the weekend was how to scare people—"

"And another," Jessica said, finishing the sentence, "is how *not* to be scared by stupid jokes like this one." She patted Lila's shoulder. "But don't worry. You'll figure that out soon enough."

Just before English class that day, Elizabeth felt something cold and wet against the back of her neck. She didn't even bother to turn around. "A wet glove on the end of a stick," she said to Amy with a yawn. "No offense or anything to whoever's doing it, but that's really pretty boring."

Amy twisted around in her seat. "Actually, Charlie," she said with a smile, "we've discovered that frozen Jell-O works much better."

"Just wrap it in a paper towel or a few tissues," Elizabeth explained in the most unexcited voice she could manage.

The cold, wet feeling stopped. Elizabeth turned around. There was Charlie, a dripping wet glove at his side. He looked totally crushed. Elizabeth looked at him and sighed.

"Bummer," she said, giving his hand a sympathetic pat. "I know how hard you must have worked to put that trick together, too."

Amy giggled. Charlie turned red and got up to change his seat. On his way, Elizabeth watched him toss the glove into the trash basket.

"Nice job!" Amy told her friend.

"It was nothing," Elizabeth said modestly.

"You didn't eat the spaghetti at lunch, did you, Brian?"

Jessica hoped she sounded convincing. She was pretty sure she did. After all, she'd had plenty of practice just yesterday.

Brian tried to elbow his way past her and into the English room. "Of course I ate the food," he said, sounding annoyed. "Why shouldn't I?"

"No reason," Jessica said with a shrug. "Of course, if you don't like maggots then that's another story—" She stepped out of his way.

But, as she expected, Brian didn't pass through. "What do you mean, if you don't like maggots?"

"There was a mix-up today," Jessica said. "One of the women who work in the cafeteria told me all about it. She wasn't really supposed to, but I asked."

"Asked what?" Brian demanded.

"Oh, I asked about those little wormy things in the spaghetti sauce," Jessica said, being careful not to smile. "Didn't you notice it tasted bad today? It certainly wasn't meat. I could tell right away. I couldn't eat more than a bite before I noticed."

"Well—" Brian began, scratching his head.

"So I asked," Jessica continued, "and the lady said they'd gotten an order of chopped-up maggots by mistake instead of meat." She fixed Brian with a look. "But it'll probably be OK, so long as you ate just a bite or two. I mean, you didn't eat all your spaghetti, did you?"

"Well—" Brian said again. He covered his mouth with his hand.

"She said most people can't tell the difference till about an hour later," Jessica said, looking at the clock, "and then they—well, they—"

"They what?" Brian demanded, frantically checking his watch.

"Well," Jessica said slowly, "she said then the maggots usually go out the same way they went in—"

"Oh, my gosh!" Brian didn't wait to hear more. He turned faintly green and went dashing down the hall.

He's as bad as Steven, Jessica thought with satisfaction. Mr. Bowman looked up in surprise as she came into the room.

"What happened to Brian?" he asked. "I thought I saw you talking to him a minute ago."

Jessica smiled her sweetest smile.

"I think something just—came up," she said.

Mandy poked Lila. "What's in the bag?" she hissed.

"Something important," Lila whispered back, careful not to interrupt Mr. Bowman as he read from an old horror story. She jerked her thumb at Aaron Dallas, who sat at the desk next to hers. "I learned my lesson at lunch today."

Mandy smiled. "Good luck."

"Thanks." Lila thought back to the awful, embarrassing scene in the cafeteria that day. She wished that Jessica and Elizabeth hadn't been quite so quick to see that the snail was a fake. *Oh, well,* she told herself. *I'll get those boys back in a few minutes. No one gets away with embarrassing Lila Fowler!*

Lila listened carefully to the story, waiting for just the right moment. It came sooner than she expected. "'Just then,'" Mr. Bowman read, his voice rising dramatically, "'the man stuck his spoon into the bowl and began to eat. He noticed that the noodles had a strange taste, but he didn't think anything of it at first.'"

Lila stole a glance at Aaron. He was wrapped up in the story, that was clear. *Good.*

She loosened the top of the bag, hoping it wouldn't crinkle too loudly.

"'Then the giant's wife came in,'" Mr. Bowman continued, "'and she said to the man, "What are you eating?"'"

On your marks, Lila thought. A rush of excitement flew through her.

"'The man looked at her in astonishment,'" Mr. Bowman went on, "'and he said: "They're noodles.'"

Get set. Her body tensed.

"'And the giant's wife looked at him, her eyes wide, and said in a soft voice: "But that bowl was where I was keeping my husband's brains!"'"

Go! With a sudden motion, Lila upset her bag of cold leftover spaghetti into Aaron's hand. For a moment, Aaron looked at it dumbly. Then he screamed.

"Calm down, calm down!" Mr. Bowman ordered, looking up at the class. "It's not *that* scary!"

Lila just sat and smiled. Within thirty seconds, Aaron had turned on the lights, tripped over a couple of desks, and flung strands of spaghetti madly around the room.

Lila smiled. *Now we're even*, she thought with satisfaction.

"What a day," Jessica sighed happily as she and Elizabeth started for home Monday afternoon.

Elizabeth nodded. "We did very well," she admitted.

"All that practicing this weekend helped," Jessica said.

Elizabeth chuckled. "They really don't have a clue."

"Boys just plain scare easier than girls," Jessica pointed out.

"I guess you're right." They approached the first corner. Jessica turned left, following the path they usually took home. "Uh—Jessica?" Elizabeth said nervously, stopping in her tracks. In the distance, she could hear a dog barking. She knew the dog well. It was fierce. It was humongous. It barked—all the time. And it was right on their usual way home, only separated from the sidewalk by a fence that really didn't seem high enough or strong enough when you thought about it. "I was just thinking," Elizabeth continued. "Today, just for a change, why don't we walk home this way instead?" She grinned widely and pointed straight down the block.

Jessica's lip curled. "Why? That's the long way around. It'd take us forever."

"Well, not really," Elizabeth argued. The dog barked again, sounding even louder and more ferocious. Elizabeth shuddered. "Just a couple of extra minutes. Just for a change, that's all. It doesn't really matter to me," she continued quickly. "I just thought—"

Jessica stared at her sister and shook her head. "All right," she agreed. "You've got something up your sleeve, don't you?"

"Oh, no!" Elizabeth said, pretending to be shocked, but she quickly hurried off across the street.

It's not that I'm afraid of it, or anything like that, she told herself, trying not to think about the part of *The Hound of the Baskervilles* she'd read during study hall that morning. The part where Sherlock Holmes was trying to figure out whether the hound was a real dog—or a real ghost.

Seven

On Tuesday morning, Steven came down to breakfast very slowly. Elizabeth and Jessica were already in the kitchen. Steven grabbed a bowl out of the dishwasher and checked it carefully. Then he opened a fresh box of cereal, just in case, and poured some into his bowl.

"Why didn't you use the old box?" Elizabeth asked him.

"Because." Steven didn't feel like explaining. He got the milk out of the refrigerator and trickled some into the bowl as slowly as he could manage.

Jessica frowned. "Some of us might like to use the milk, too, you know."

Steven snorted. "Some of us might like to make it through the week without being tortured by stupid tricks. For a change." He finished pouring and stirred his cereal several more times, checking for mysterious lumps.

"I've got a great idea, Jess," Elizabeth said to her sister. "Let's have a slumber party on Friday and invite everyone over."

"Why Friday?" Jessica wanted to know.

Elizabeth's eyes danced. "Because it's Friday the Thirteenth."

"Terrific!" Jessica exclaimed. "We can make it a victory party, too."

"Victory party for what?" Steven grumbled, opening the newspaper to check out the latest sports scores.

The girls looked at each other and burst into laughter. "What's so funny?" Steven demanded. He brought the bowl and the paper over to the table, carefully checking the seat of his chair before he sat down.

"Victory over the boys, of course," Jessica replied. "I mean, we're *definitely* going to win."

"What are you talking about?" Steven asked, tasting his first mouthful. It seemed to be OK, so he swallowed it.

"You helped us win, you know," Elizabeth told him. "Maybe I should do something nice for you— bake you cookies or something."

Steven's eyes bugged out. Before he knew what he was doing, he was out of his seat, sputtering on his cereal. "Don't you dare!" he cried.

"I'd give that one an eight," Jessica said. "How about you?"

"Only a seven," Elizabeth argued. Steven sat down slowly, shaking his head. "But seriously, Steven, you helped us more than you know," Elizabeth went on. She winked at Jessica. "If you want to come to our slumber party, you'd be more than welcome."

"Who, me? Not on your life," Steven grumbled. "I plan to be in Timbuktu that weekend. I can't think of anything much scarier than a bunch of twelve-year-olds staying up till way past their bed-time."

"I can!" Jessica said, breaking up into laughter again. Steven wondered what was going on. Was there a rubber mouse bleeding to death on the floor somewhere? Cautiously he checked under his chair. Nothing.

"Hey, I'm serious," he said, thrusting his spoon into the cereal. "By the way, have you heard this one? 'Knock, knock,'" he began, realizing he hadn't told his sisters the joke he'd made up Saturday morning.

"Sorry, Steven, but we don't have time to tell knock-knock jokes with you," Jessica told him. "We've got to go to school. Come on, Lizzie!" The girls raced from the house, laughing loudly. "'Bye, Steven! Watch out for plastic spiders!" Jessica called behind her.

"A tape recorder," Steven said sourly to himself. "A tape recorder? Aaaaah!" *Let's face it*, he told himself, *it's a pretty stupid joke.*

Steven sat silently and ate his cereal. But as he drained the last drop from his bowl, he began to smile. He hated the whole idea of a slumber party, but maybe it would all work to his advantage.

It's spelled R-E-V-E-N-G-E, he told himself with a grin. *And if I do things right, it'll sure taste sweet!*

"What a great day," Jessica sighed as she walked home from school on Tuesday with Mandy.

"I know it," Mandy agreed, grinning. "Now we know that Bruce Patman believes in ghosts."

"Well, at least he believes in helium balloons that have white sheets taped to them," Jessica amended.

"When they're sailed into a dark bathroom," Mandy continued, beginning to snicker. "I didn't know he could yell so loudly."

Jessica giggled. "Did they pull any stunts at all—on any of the girls?"

"Well, they certainly tried," Mandy said with a laugh. "The bloody feet in the bathroom stall, the tape-recorded gunshots when Lila bent over—" She ticked them off on her fingers. "But none of them worked. The best of all was the computer room."

"Tell me," Jessica urged.

"Charlie was working on one of the terminals," Mandy explained, "and Elizabeth figured out how to send a message from her terminal to his. So we're all on one side of the room, right?"

"Uh-huh," Jessica said, growing interested.

"And we're all watching Charlie," Mandy continued. "And suddenly you can see Charlie stiffen, like he's just had an electric shock, and someone says to him: 'What's the matter, Charlie?'"

"And then?" Jessica said.

Mandy smiled. "And then Charlie went over to the teacher and asked permission to move to a new terminal for the rest of the period."

"Great!" Jessica exclaimed. "What was the message?"

"'They're coming to get you, Charlie!'" Mandy told her. "And Elizabeth did it so the only way to erase it was to shut the terminal off."

"What a day!" Jessica repeated, grinning from ear to ear.

Quite late Tuesday night, Elizabeth put down *The Hound of the Baskervilles* and sighed happily. Finished at last. *What a wonderful book*, she thought. And not a bit scary. "I can't imagine why anyone would call this scary," she murmured as she turned off the light. "I mean, the hound doesn't even turn out to be a real ghost." Still, Elizabeth reached out in the darkness and switched on her radio. Nice and low. Comforting music, that was all, just something to make it easier to go to sleep.

"Anyone home?" Jessica called loudly on Wednesday afternoon, walking in the front door and throwing down her schoolbooks.

There was no answer. *Oh, yeah—Mom and Dad are working,* Jessica reminded herself, *and Elizabeth's staying late at school to work on the newspaper, and Steven's got basketball practice.* Feeling brave, she picked up her book of Poe stories and settled down on the couch to read another one.

"Let's see," she muttered as she thumbed through. "'Hop-Frog'—no—'The Masque of the Red Death'—I don't think so—'The Tell-Tale Heart'?" *Sounds good,* she told herself. *Plus, it's short.*

The story told of some dead guy, and the narrator seemed to think that the dead guy's heart was still beating. Just for company, Jessica got up and switched on the television set.

A commercial jingle came on, something about the "Heartbeat of America." Jessica had heard it hundreds of times. Somehow she didn't want to hear it today. Hastily she changed the channel.

The Phyllis Hartley talk show. *Hearts again.* Jessica shuddered and clicked once more.

"Do you have an irregular heartbeat?" a newscaster demanded. With a sigh, Jessica got up and turned the television off. Picking up the book, she read another page or two before deciding that she didn't feel like doing homework when she was alone in the house. After all, there was still plenty of time to do the assignment.

Anyway, she told herself, *another story might be more—more interesting.*

*　　　*　　　*

Elizabeth overslept a little on Thursday morning. When she awoke, she sat bolt upright. *What was that?* It sounded like the baying of an enormous hound! Elizabeth jumped out of bed and was halfway to the door when she stopped in her tracks.

Just Steven singing in the shower, she told herself ruefully, shaking her head and sitting back down on her bed. *Off-key as usual.* She rubbed her eyes and took a deep breath.

Nothing to worry about.

What a bunch of wimps, Jessica thought after school on Thursday. The boys hadn't tried a thing all day—not one single solitary trick. She was almost disappointed.

A total easy victory. She smiled to herself, walking into one of the conference rooms in the school library.

Maybe too easy.

Just to be sure, Jessica closed the door to the conference room. She relaxed in a chair and flipped her Poe book out of her backpack. Mr. Bowman had mentioned a story in class today, and Jessica thought she'd try that one. *Let's see,* she wondered, scanning the table of contents, *what was it called? "The Cask of—Amontiyado," wasn't that right?* Jessica located the page and realized the word was spelled "Amontillado." *Pretty weird,* she said with a shrug, and she settled down to read.

Amontillado turned out to be a kind of wine. The narrator, who was named Montresor, was inviting a friend of his over to taste some special kind of wine he had. *Why would anybody want to see some stupid wine?* Jessica wondered impatiently. *Now, if it were fancy clothes instead—*

For some reason, Montresor was keeping the wine in a back room that seemed a little like a cave. A crypt, Poe called it. Jessica read on. The two men went farther and farther down into the crypt until they finally came to the barrel full of the wine. Jessica paused for a moment. For some reason, she seemed to be biting her fingernails. Swallowing hard, she sat on her hands and forced her eyes to return to the page.

In the story, Montresor made his "friend" crawl into the little tiny space where the wine was kept. *You fool!* Jessica thought, mentally urging the other man to stay away. *He's planning something, and I bet there's no other way out of that space—*

Abruptly Jessica looked around. Was it her imagination, or was the ceiling getting lower? Wasn't the conference room growing darker? *And what was that noise on the other side of the door?*

Quickly Jessica stood up and flung the door to the room wide open. She breathed deeply. *Good old library air!* Laughing a little, Jessica walked into the main library. *What an imagination,* she told herself. *You actually thought the conference room was a cave!*

As Jessica looked for a table where other kids

were sitting, she sighed. *Old Mr. Poe's not so scary*, she assured herself. *I just don't feel comfortable inside those conference rooms.*

But she chose a seat where she could see the door to the library, just in case.

"It looks like all the Unicorns can come," Jessica said Thursday night. She and Elizabeth were sitting at their dining room table before dinner, planning their slumber party.

"OK," Elizabeth said. "Amy and Maria can make it, too. It should be a great party."

In the kitchen, Steven overheard their conversation. He grinned wickedly. *It should be great, all right!*

"If you get some videos," Jessica continued, "I'll take care of some refreshments."

"Brownies," Elizabeth suggested.

"Of course, brownies," Jessica agreed, "and ice cream, and marshmallows—do you think we can roast marshmallows over the stove burners?"

"Probably not," Steven heard Elizabeth say.

"Well, maybe we'll think of something," Jessica went on. "It should be totally fun. Mom and Dad are going out to a party and won't be back till late. And Steven won't be home either. What a relief!"

Yeah? Well, the same to you, Steven thought, irritated.

"Really?" came Elizabeth's voice. "Where's he going?"

Don't you wish you knew, Steven thought, a twinkle in his eye.

"I. D. K. and I. D. C.," Jessica told her.

"What's that mean?"

"I don't know and I don't care," Jessica said with a giggle.

In the kitchen Steven sat back, a smile of satisfaction on his face. *You may not know, sister dear*, he chuckled to himself, *but you're going to care, all right!*

Oh, boy, are you ever going to care!

Eight

◇

At five o'clock Friday afternoon, Steven picked up a couple of volleyballs and headed for the front door.

"See you later!" he called out. "I'm out of here!"

"Don't hurry back!" Jessica cried out over the roar of the vacuum cleaner. She was cleaning the living room.

"Are you sure you don't want to stay?" Elizabeth asked, a twinkle in her eye. She came to the door and stuck a sign on it that read "ABANDON HOPE ALL YE WHO ENTER HERE." "Some of your favorite people are coming." She batted her eyelashes at Steven.

Steven gritted his teeth. "In your dreams," he told her. "Thanks anyway. I'll pass."

"Where are you going?" Elizabeth asked curiously.

Steven smiled. "Oh, off to shoot a few baskets."

"With a volleyball?" Elizabeth asked.

Oops. "It's a new game," Steven told her, trying hard not to crack a smile. "You play it like volleyball, but you use a basketball court. If you serve the ball into the opponent's basket, you get an extra five points."

"Oh." Elizabeth nodded. "And if someone intercepts it, they can run it back for a touchdown?"

"That's right," Steven said slowly, not sure if he was being kidded or not. "It's the hottest thing at the high school. Well, I'll be seeing you." *And sooner than you think,* he added to himself. Whistling, he threw the bag with the volleyballs over his shoulder and walked out the door.

Steven walked a few yards down the sidewalk, just in case anyone was watching from the house. Then he turned around and cut quietly through a neighbor's yard. Soon he was standing outside his own garage.

Humming the latest Johnny Buck single to himself, Steven emptied the bag and tossed the volleyballs gently into the garage. "Gotcha!" he hummed. *What did Jessica mean, he sang off-key? Why, he was almost as good as Johnny Buck himself!* "I'm gonna getcha, gonna getcha—Gotcha!"

Next, Steven checked the house one more time. No one was watching. Good. Now for the tricky part. Steven walked around the house till he came to the basement window he'd purposely left open.

He held his breath and slid through. Kicking his feet, he landed safely on top of the dryer.

"Gonna getcha, gonna getcha," he hummed happily, shutting the window behind him. Steven walked across the basement and up the steps that led to the first floor. He turned the bolt so it couldn't be opened from upstairs. *Excellent*, he told himself.

Finally Steven walked over to a table he'd set up in the middle of the basement. All the materials were there, ready for him to create a masterpiece. *A few more hours*, he told himself. He rubbed his hands in anticipation. It might take that long to put his masterpiece together—but it would be worth it. Oh, boy, would it be worth it!

"Gonna getcha, gonna getcha—" he hummed. . . . *Gotcha!*

Amy and Maria were the first guests to arrive. Jessica greeted them at the door. She was dressed in a ratty old jacket she'd found in the coat closet, and she'd added lipstick and eyebrow pencil across her face to make it look like she'd been hacked to pieces. "Greetings!" she called out in her best Mr. Bowman imitation. "Come in, and don't look back!"

Giggling, Amy and Maria made it into the living room, where Elizabeth met them with a pitcher of something red in one hand. "Care for something from one of the four food groups?" she asked.

Amy wrinkled her brow. "Cereal, meat, vegetables, and—?" she questioned.

"Don't be silly," Elizabeth replied, keeping a straight face. "Don't you remember science last term? Blood comes in four types: A, B, O, and AB. Which type would you like?" She held out the pitcher.

Maria smiled. "I thought the four food groups were brownies, marshmallows, ice cream, and candy bars."

Jessica came in from the door with Lila and Janet. "You're right, Maria," she said. "Lucky we've got plenty of them all!"

The party was a terrific success. The girls went through an entire freezer full of ice cream in less than two hours. They watched *Friday the Thirteenth: Part XXXVI* on videotape, shrieking for fun at all the scary parts. "This is sure a lot scarier than those stupid stories Mr. Bowman was making us read," Lila said, covering her eyes with a pillow.

Jessica watched the screen, fascinated. Somehow, after reading several stories by Edgar Allan Poe— well, all right, after reading one story by Edgar Allan Poe and parts of two others—*Friday the Thirteenth: Part XXXVI* didn't seem nearly as spooky as she'd expected. But she wasn't about to say so. "You are so right, Lila," she said.

"Eeeek!" Amy screeched. "Look at the size of that knife!"

On the screen the killer plunged the knife down

into the victim's heart. *Yuk,* Jessica thought as she watched the blood pouring out. *Of course, that's not real blood,* she reminded herself. To her surprise, she found her thoughts were wandering. Instead of screaming along with the others, she was wondering whether the moviemakers had used ketchup or spaghetti sauce.

On the whole, she thought critically, remembering the scares they'd experienced over the last week, she would recommend spaghetti sauce.

"All right, who floated the bloody hand in the toilet?" Mary Wallace demanded, coming out of the bathroom a few minutes later.

Jessica pretended surprise. "Now, who would do a thing like that?"

"You would," Mary said sourly.

Jessica smiled. "We wouldn't want to lose our touch, you know."

"That's right." Elizabeth sat down on the couch next to her sister and picked up a handful of popcorn, checking it for rubber worms first. "After all," she said with a frown, "those boys never surrendered, did they?"

Jessica shook her head. "But don't worry about it," she told her twin. "After what we did to them this week, I bet they won't even show their faces at school on Monday."

"If you say so." Elizabeth sighed and stretched out her feet.

"I know so." Jessica wiggled around and sat down

again—right onto something cold and sticky! "Yikes!" she cried, jumping up again quickly and slapping her hand against her bottom. "What's that?"

"A bowl of ice cream," Janet said, a wicked grin on her face. "Like you said, Jessica, we wouldn't want to lose our touch."

Looks like a storm is brewing outside, Elizabeth said to herself as she turned off the last video at eleven o'clock. She listened to the wind blow across the windows and shivered. "Come on, guys," she called out, "let's get our sleeping bags ready and tell some ghost stories."

Jessica put the leftover brownies in the middle of the floor. One by one, the guests unrolled their sleeping bags into a circle. "How about getting a candle, Lizzie?" Jessica asked brightly.

"That's a great idea!" Elizabeth replied. She found a big one and lighted it. Then she turned off the light and put the candle next to the plate of brownies. *It looks kind of spooky,* she told herself, *but at least we're all here together.* The living room had a big picture window that overlooked the backyard. From where Elizabeth sat on her sleeping bag, she could see straight out through it. It felt a little better to know that she could see any ghosts that might be prowling around the house.

Or any hounds.

Not that there were any ghosts or bloodthirsty hounds, of course.

The room seemed awfully quiet all of a sudden. Elizabeth spoke up. "So who'd like to tell us a ghost story?" Her voice seemed unnaturally loud in the stillness.

"How about Maria?" Amy suggested.

Elizabeth looked at Maria. "Go ahead," she said.

"All right." Maria nodded and took a deep breath. "This is the story of Tobias McComish," she said in a half-whisper.

"Tobias who?" Jessica asked in a strangely high voice.

"Tobias McComish," Maria went on softly. "Tobias McComish was a kind and gentle man who owned a lakefront cottage in Canada. The lake was off in the middle of nowhere, and in order to get there you either had to paddle a canoe or else figure out how to land in a helicopter." She paused and looked around at her audience.

"I don't see what's so scary about this story," Janet said.

"Wait," Maria told her. "One night the neighbors heard some terrible screams coming from the McComish cottage. They ran over there and searched the place, but they could find no one." Elizabeth felt a small tingle begin at the base of her spine and work its way up her back. "The only weird thing they saw was something that looked like a small carrot lying on the ground. It looked like it had been covered with ketchup."

"Ketchup!" Jessica scoffed. "Give me a break!"

But Elizabeth noticed that her twin leaned even closer toward Maria.

"All right, spaghetti sauce," Maria amended. "Anyway, for the next few days, Tobias McComish didn't appear." Maria pulled the ends of her sleeping bag up closer to her shoulders. "The neighbors called his house in the city. No one answered. Then they called his office. Tobias hadn't come back to work—even though his vacation was over."

"And what happened then?" Ellen asked, squirming in her sleeping bag.

Maria looked from one girl to the next. "Finally, one neighbor went over to Tobias's cottage again," she said at last. Elizabeth could hear the wind howling a little louder. "It was dark, and the moon was full. As he walked through the front door, he felt as if someone was watching him. He started looking around, calling Tobias's name. For a while there was no answer. And then—" Maria paused dramatically.

Elizabeth felt that prickle of fear again. No one said a word.

"Suddenly Tobias McComish came floating down the steps from the attic," Maria said loudly. "It took just one look to see that he wasn't alive, he was a ghost! And there was red stuff dripping from the end of his fingers, and he was moaning 'Bloody Fingers! Bloo-oo-oody Fingers!'"

Elizabeth felt Amy clutch her hand.

"The neighbor ran out of there in a hurry,"

Maria went on, staring directly at the flickering candle. "The next night another neighbor went in. She saw and heard the same thing: Tobias McComish's ghost, crying 'Bloody Fingers! Bloo-oo-oody Fingers!'"

If I close my eyes, Elizabeth realized, *I can almost see the ghost coming down the stairs.* She opened her eyes as wide as she possibly could.

"Next the sheriff went into the McComish place," Maria said. "And when he saw the same thing, he didn't stick around for long: 'Bloody Fingers!' he heard the ghost calling. 'Bloo-oo-oody Fingers!'"

Elizabeth pulled her forehead up to make sure her eyes didn't close.

"For a few months, no one went into the McComish cabin," Maria went on. "But then one day, a little girl decided to go and see the ghost."

"She was pretty stupid," Lila commented.

"She was pretty brave," Maria corrected her. "And that night, just like always, Tobias McComish came floating down the stairs toward her, calling out 'Bloody Fingers!'"

Elizabeth shuddered. Maria's voice seemed to be getting even spookier.

"But the girl didn't run," Maria continued. "She just stood there. And the ghost came closer and said menacingly, 'Bloody Fingers!'"

"I think I'd like another brownie," Jessica said to no one in particular.

"And when the girl still didn't run away, Tobias McComish came even closer and said: 'Bloody Fingers! Bloo-oo-oody Fingers!' And this time, he held up his hands—or what had once been his hands."

"Ugh," Amy whispered.

"And the little girl looked and saw that red stuff on Tobias McComish's hands," Maria said. "But she still didn't run away. Instead, she looked straight at him and said—"

Suddenly Maria made a lunge toward Elizabeth. Something long and thin came flying directly at her!

Elizabeth screamed. She tried to dodge, but she was too late. The object hit her in the side and landed in her lap. *It's just like a finger*, she told herself in horror—*a wet, bloody finger!*

All over the room there were screams. Mandy and Janet jumped out of their sleeping bags, and Janet and Ellen were clutching each other. Then Maria's strong voice took command. "That girl looked straight at Tobias McComish and said to him: 'Well, if you have bloody fingers, why don't you put on a Band-Aid?'"

For a moment Elizabeth stared at her friend. The room was suddenly silent. Janet let go of Ellen's arms. Finally, Elizabeth burst out laughing. "A Band-Aid. Of course! So what's this?" She poked at the "finger" beside her.

"It's a carrot stick," Maria confessed. "I brought

it from home—I thought it might be a good prop for telling a story. But I bet you thought—"

"Yes, whatever," Janet interrupted quickly, getting ahold of herself. "So who wants to go next?"

"My turn!" Elizabeth volunteered. She launched into a retelling of the *Hound of the Baskervilles*.

Halfway through the story, there was a flash of lightning. Ellen gasped.

Elizabeth turned around—and gasped herself. Another flash of lightning followed the first. There, silhouetted on the wall, were four monstrous shadows. Worse, the four monstrous shadows were moving. "They're outside," Elizabeth could hear Lila murmur, in a voice that didn't sound much like Lila's own.

"I'm going to scream," Jessica threatened.

"No, you don't," Elizabeth ordered, reaching across the circle and clapping her hand over her sister's mouth. "Let's get a little closer and see what's going on." *Whatever they are*, she thought bravely, *there are about fifteen of us and only four of them.*

At least, I hope there are only four of them.

Elizabeth crawled over to the picture window, hoping to stay well out of sight of whatever might be in the yard. Several other girls followed her. There was no moon, and the storm was getting worse. "Let's just wait for the next lightning bolt," Elizabeth whispered. Maria, next to her, nodded grimly.

Elizabeth dug her fingernails into the frame of

the window and hoisted herself up slowly. *What on earth is out there?* she asked herself. She decided she would rather know—no matter how terrible it might be—than to stay in suspense like this. Straining to see out, Elizabeth could hear Lila whimpering behind her.

All at once a huge flash of lightning lit up the yard. Elizabeth caught her breath. Outside there were two ghosts, a skeleton, and something else she couldn't quite recognize. A scream rose in Elizabeth's throat.

But something stopped her. Elizabeth grabbed tighter to the frame and tried to adjust her eyes to the darkness. What had she just seen?

"What is it, Elizabeth?" Jessica asked shakily behind her.

Another beam of lightning struck. What was that line in *The Hound of the Baskervilles*? "They were the footprints of a gigantic hound!" she quoted. *Feet, that was it.* In the glow Elizabeth could clearly see the fourth figure. *A mummy*, she thought, but she forced herself to concentrate on the figure's feet. *Aha.*

"I really am going to scream," Janet threatened from behind her.

Elizabeth whirled around. "Hush, all of you!" she hissed. "Do mummies wear Nikes?"

There was a moment's pause. Then Jessica and Lila pushed their way to the window and peered out.

"Of course," Jessica said after a moment. "It's so obvious."

"It's just Brian and Charlie," Lila said, beginning to giggle.

"And Aaron and Bruce," Jessica added. "What a lame way to try to scare us."

"I'll say," Janet agreed from the back of the room. "I wasn't fooled for a minute."

"Let's laugh at them," Amy suggested. "What do you say, Elizabeth?"

But Elizabeth was barely listening. She was furious—angrier than she could remember being for weeks. *The nerve of those boys!* she thought. *Trying to scare us outside my own house!* An idea began to form in her mind. "We're not just going to laugh at them," she said decisively.

Jessica and Lila turned toward her, frowning. "What do you mean?" Lila demanded.

"We're going to give them the scare of their lives," Elizabeth told her, clenching her fists. "We're going to make those boys beg for mercy!"

Nine

Down in the basement, Steven checked the luminous dial of his wristwatch. *Almost time*, he told himself. *And a good thing, too*. It was hard for an active guy like him to sit still for long. But it was all for a good cause. Anything to get back at those bratty little sisters of his.

Steven shifted position. He looked through the materials on the table in front of him and picked up— the knife. Steven chuckled. It was a large knife, and it gleamed in the little light that was in the basement.

A few more minutes, and everything would be ready.

He could hardly wait.

"So what's your idea, Elizabeth?" Jessica asked, wishing she'd thought of one first.

Elizabeth began slowly. "Well, it's from the story I was telling—*The Hound of the Baskervilles*."

Jessica rolled her eyes. "Oh, come on. How is a book that's three centuries old going to help us scare those boys?"

"It's only one century old," Elizabeth corrected her. "And I think it will work. The hound in the story isn't a real ghost," she explained. "It's a regular dog, a humongous dog. But the catch is, the villain has painted a terrible face on the dog so it looks much fiercer than it really is."

"I get it!" Amy said enthusiastically. "So we paint a scary face on—" Then she stopped. Jessica thought she could see Amy's face turn into a frown.

"But you don't have a dog, Elizabeth," Amy finished.

"I know we don't," Elizabeth said, "but we don't need one. We'll paint a scary face on the side of my sleeping bag."

"You're crazy," Jessica objected. "That wouldn't fool anybody."

"Do you have a better idea?" Elizabeth challenged her.

Did she have a better idea? She had to admit, she didn't. "All right," she muttered with a sigh. "But don't blame me if it doesn't work out."

"Do you have glow-in-the-dark paints?" Mandy asked.

Elizabeth frowned. "I guess I hadn't thought about—"

"Yes, we do," Jessica cut in triumphantly, looking straight at Mandy. She turned to Elizabeth. "Don't you remember?" she asked her sister. "When we went out shopping for all the stuff we would need to trick Steven, that was one of the things we bought. I guess we never got around to using it."

"Jessica!" Elizabeth said gleefully. "You're brilliant!"

"Thank you, thank you," Jessica said, blowing kisses to the other girls. "I'll go get them—and some brushes."

"Won't the boys see what's going on?" Ellen asked.

"No way," Jessica told her breezily. Elizabeth's project suddenly felt like her own. "We're OK as long as it doesn't get any lighter out."

"My sleeping bag is a pretty dark blue," Elizabeth pointed out. "The boys won't see it against the sky. If we can make the fangs bloody enough, it ought to work."

"But we'd better hurry," Jessica added. She looked over toward the window and shuddered. "There's no telling what those losers are up to. They could attack at any moment."

Downstairs, Steven spun around. *What was that clanking noise?*

He held his breath and listened carefully. It sounded a little like someone escaping from a jail cell.

They weren't planning a trick on him, were they? No one had been watching when he climbed through the basement window, he was pretty sure of that. He'd been quiet ever since, putting the things together that he needed, and he'd worked with hardly any light. He hadn't even sneezed! And certainly no one had come downstairs. *They wouldn't dare*, Steven told himself with a grin, *unless there were at least six of them, anyway. How many sixth-grade girls does it take to go down into the basement? Ten. One to open the door and nine to scream. Hmm. Not bad.*

Now that he listened carefully, he could tell the noise wasn't coming from upstairs at all—it was outside.

Steven crept slowly over to the basement window, aware that his heart was beating faster than usual. Careful to keep himself hidden, he stared outside.

Huh?

Steven rubbed his eyes. He pictured himself trying to explain this one to Cathy, his girlfriend. "Honest, Cathy, then I looked up and there was this crazy kid dressed as a mummy standing in my backyard, and he was banging together a couple of blades from an old airplane propeller!" *Right.* She'd probably try to have him locked up.

Behind the mummy Steven could just make out three other figures. A skeleton, a couple of ghosts. He recognized them, too. *Great*, he thought. *Some dumb middle schoolers trying to put a stupid scare into my sisters and their friends. Well, if they're still around when I go into my act, then they'll see what a real expert can do.* He began to cheer up. *I'll take it to Hollywood. I'll call it—Steven Gets Even!*

Maybe that would be the next hit Johnny Buck song. "Steven Gets Even!" He imagined Johnny himself singing his song in concert. How would it go? He sang in a soft voice, careful not to be heard upstairs.

> "The poor guy had some sisters who were rotten and mean—
> So he set up the grisliest, scariest scene—
> Those girls ran till they were hardly breathin',
> And you know what he called it? 'Steven Gets Even!'"

Well, I can work on it later, maybe. With an evil smile, Steven began walking back to the table to work on the last part of his plan:

The blood.

"Ready?" Elizabeth whispered a few minutes later. She opened the front door a crack.

"Ready," Mandy hissed.

Elizabeth took a deep breath. "On the count of three, OK? One—" Her heart was hammering. "Two—"

The back of the line began to move. "Three!" Elizabeth said, louder than she'd meant to, and then she shoved the door wide open.

"AAAAAH!" A crowd of screaming girls dashed out of the house and scattered in all directions. "Aaaaah!" Elizabeth screamed as if her life depended on it. Close behind came Jessica, Maria, and Mandy, their faces hidden by the Horrible Thing of Sweet Valley. It looked so monstrous that Elizabeth didn't want to be anywhere near it.

Elizabeth watched as the two ghosts screamed and ran directly into each other. Mixed with her own and her friends' screams, she thought she recognized Aaron's voice.

"Help! Help! Get it off me!"

"Save me!" wailed the other ghost, rolling on the ground.

They can't even see where they're going, Elizabeth thought with a grin. *Should've used bigger eyeholes.* With a flying leap she landed right on top of the two ghosts. *Yup, Aaron,* she told herself happily. *And let me see, this one's—Bruce.*

"I want to go home!" Bruce sobbed.

Lights snapped on in windows all over the neighborhood.

"Owoooooo!" howled Mandy and Maria and Jessica, carrying the sleeping bag.

"Aaaah!" shrieked Aaron and Bruce.

"Quiet!" yelled the nosy neighbor down the block, banging down his window in disgust.

That takes care of Bruce and Aaron, Elizabeth thought with satisfaction. *How about Brian and Charlie?*

"Food! Food! Give us food!" Jessica chanted in her most unearthly voice. She was grinning from ear to ear. *This is the best time I've had in weeks,* she thought as she ran after the boy dressed in a skeleton costume. *We should do this every day!* "Foo-oo-ood!"

The heavy chains that were draped around the boy clanked and rattled. He screamed and ran faster.

"Human flesh!" Mandy shouted. "Feed me!"

"No more bloody fingers!" Maria added in her low actress's voice.

Clanking and shrieking with terror, the skeleton fell to the ground. The girls bounded over to him.

"Don't let that thing near me!" he whimpered, trying to pick himself up. But it was no use. Together, Mandy, Jessica, and Maria piled on top of him.

It's Brian, Jessica thought with satisfaction.

"This is the end!" Maria boomed out directly into his ear. Jessica thought she'd never heard anyone cry so loudly.

"I surrender!" Brian cried, covering his ears. "Don't kill me!"

Jessica began to giggle. "Talk about wimpy," she said to the other girls.

"Yeah, this is almost too easy," Mandy agreed.

Timidly, Brian peeked up at the three girls.

Jessica waved her hand in front of his face. "Hi, Brian," she said, batting her eyelashes. "Remember me?"

"Here's Brian," Mandy announced a few minutes later, shoving him through the front door.

"That makes three," Elizabeth said. "So where's the mummy?"

Mandy scratched her head. "He probably got away."

Janet looked around at the three boys. "That must have been Charlie," she said with a sniff. "It's a wonder he didn't unwind and trip over his own bandages."

"His own toilet paper bandages," Elizabeth amended with a giggle.

"Jessica and Maria are still out there, just in case," Mandy said, pushing Brian firmly onto the couch next to the other boys. "If he turns up again, they'll get him."

It's funny, Elizabeth thought, *but I can't remember seeing Charlie.* She tried to think back to the moment when they'd rushed out of the door. Aaron and Bruce had gone one way, Brian another, and as for Charlie—

I don't know, she thought uneasily. Somehow, she didn't like the idea of Jessica and Maria out there all by themselves. Leaving the other girls to take charge of their prisoners, she slipped quietly out the front door.

"I'll check the driveway," Maria suggested.

"OK," Jessica agreed. "But I don't think he's anywhere near here."

Maria laughed. "I bet you're right. It's funny, though—I didn't see him take off. Did you?"

Jessica shook her head. She couldn't remember seeing the mummy anywhere. "He probably took off the second he saw the Thing," she said with a laugh. "I'll check around the tree."

"OK," Maria told her. "I'll meet you inside, afterwards."

Jessica nodded and walked over toward the tree. It looked perfectly normal from the front. She stepped around the trunk. Nothing behind it, either. *OK*, she told herself. *Whoever he was, he's gone. And a good thing too.*

She turned back toward the house—and gasped. A ghostly foot was hanging out of the tree, right in front of her face!

Jessica stifled a scream and shut her eyes. When she opened them again, the mummy stood directly in front of her. "You were in the tree the whole time," she blurted out, feeling her heart pounding a mile a minute.

The mummy smiled. "I am cursed," it whispered in a horrifying voice, "and so will you be cursed!" It raised its arms threateningly.

It's only some dumb boy, who thinks he's being scary, Jessica told herself. But for some reason, her heart was pounding. Then, out of the corner of her eye, she saw someone approaching.

Good old Elizabeth! she thought happily.

He's really something! Elizabeth thought, peering at Charlie the mummy. She had arrived outside just as the mummy had dropped out of the tree. *Who does he think he is, trying to scare Jessica like this? Hasn't he figured out by now that girls rule?*

Elizabeth looked around her. How would she get revenge? Rocks? No; she didn't want to hurt Charlie, just get him to leave Jessica alone. Push him into the pool? No—*Aha!*

She sprinted to the side of the house, grabbed the garden hose, and turned on the water full blast. *Oh boy, is this ever going to be fun!*

"Elizabeth?" Elizabeth jumped for a moment, but then she recognized Maria's voice. "What's going on?"

Elizabeth pointed to the tree. "We're going to give Mr. Charlie Cashman a lesson he won't soon forget. Come on!" She pulled on the hose and ran straight at Charlie.

Maria followed. "Aim it carefully," she advised. "You don't want to soak Jessica, too."

"Don't worry." Elizabeth took a deep breath and held her finger down over the nozzle.

As the first drops hit Charlie, he spun around. "Hey, what the—?"

"Water brigade!" Elizabeth shouted, aiming right at Charlie's head.

"Awesome!" Jessica stepped back. "Thanks, Lizzie!" she shouted. "You saved the day!"

"Ow! Help!" Charlie called, struggling to avoid the water.

Elizabeth giggled as she focused the spray onto Charlie's back. "I always said Charlie Cashman was all wet," she observed.

"Ow!" Charlie screamed. "It's cold!" Water gushed across his head and chest.

"Ugh." Maria sniffed. "His toilet paper is coming apart."

"Stop torturing me!" Charlie pleaded. He tried to run, but his feet slipped on the wet grass and he fell sideways. By now he was a mass of tangled, wet paper. Elizabeth stepped forward and trained the end of the hose straight down on him. "Give up?" she asked, her eyes twinkling.

Charlie only sputtered.

"Suit yourself." Laughing, Elizabeth gave the hose a little shake.

"Stop, stop," Charlie begged at last, gasping for breath.

"Well, OK, I guess you're wet enough for now," Elizabeth relented, aiming the hose in the opposite direction. "Are you *sure* you give up?"

Charlie was coughing and nodding vigorously as he got to his feet. "You win," he said. "I'm giving up."

"That's better," Elizabeth said, examining him from head to toe. There were leaves stuck to his shirt, and his hair was plastered down as if he'd been swimming. *In a way, I guess he has*, Elizabeth thought proudly.

"Gonna getcha," she sang, and her twin joined in. "Gonna, getcha, gonna getcha—"

Together, they pointed at Charlie.

"Gotcha!"

"What brave boys you are!" Janet said when Charlie was brought in. Aaron, Bruce, and Brian were still huddled on the couch. "Want to see what you ran from?"

"No," Aaron said with an emphatic shake of the head.

"Uh-uh," Bruce said softly. Brian just looked at the floor.

"Too bad," Janet told them. "Meet the 'Thing of Sweet Valley'! Ta-dah!" She stretched out her arms like a game show host, as Jessica and Maria carried the girls' monster forward.

Bruce, Brian, and Aaron just gaped at it.

"Don't you have anything to say?" Elizabeth asked sweetly.

"I know, I know," Jessica interrupted, before the boys had a chance to speak a word. "It's a wonderful work of art, and this creature ought to star in the next Friday the Thirteenth movie."

Bruce stared at it, looking stunned.

"How did you—" Aaron began.

"That thing didn't scare me for a minute," Charlie scoffed. Jessica reached over and patted his hand. "OK, have it your way. You weren't scared at all." She rolled her eyes. *Boys.*

"Boys are just plain cowards, aren't they?" Janet said.

"Not nearly as brave as girls," Jessica agreed with a smile. "It's a known fact. It's in the genes or something. Don't you remember—we learned about it in science class?"

Brian shook his head. "We did not."

Jessica gave an exaggerated sigh. "All right," she said. "Just wait till we tell everyone at school that you practically wet your pants when you saw Elizabeth's sleeping bag."

"We did not either practically wet our pants!" Brian protested.

Jessica shrugged. "Maybe you didn't," she said, "but you wouldn't like it if I told people you did, now would you?"

The boys looked at each other. At last Bruce sighed. "OK," he said with a shake of the head. "You win."

"Sign a public statement?" Charlie gasped a few minutes later. "Are you out of your minds?"

Elizabeth just smiled. "Of course you'll have to sign," she told the boys. "You lost, didn't you?" She got a piece of paper and a red pen. "Ah, the color of blood," she told the other girls happily.

"But—" Aaron argued.

Elizabeth interrupted. "I hereby agree," she said, reading as she wrote, "that we boys have seriously lost the Scare War and are much worse at scare tactics than girls. Signed—"

"Wait," Maria objected. "There need to be other penalties, too."

"Like what?" Elizabeth asked.

Maria looked thoughtful. "We should make them cluck like chickens for a little while," she said at last, a grin spreading across her face.

"I like it!" Elizabeth said, writing quickly. *And I further agree to cluck like a chicken for*—"Thirty seconds?" she suggested.

"Make it a minute," Janet said.

"A minute sounds fine," Elizabeth said, finishing the sentence.

"Hey, that's not fair!" Brian protested, looking around the room. No one said anything. "I mean—" Then he sighed. "All right. I guess."

Elizabeth smiled at him. She had to admit, she was just a little bit sorry for the boys. Not much, of course. Just a tiny bit.

"OK," she announced. "Cluck like chickens. Anything else?"

Amy twirled her finger through her hair. "I think they need to address us by a special title all next week at school," she suggested.

"That's a great idea!" Maria nodded. "Like 'Your Majesty' or something."

"'Your Majesty' isn't grand enough," Lila complained.

"What can be grander than being a queen?"

Jessica wanted to know. "Hey! How about 'Your Greatness'?"

"Boring," Janet told her. "I like 'O Great and Mighty Unicorn.'" She turned expectantly toward the others. Ellen and Lila were already beginning to nod.

"But we're not all Unicorns," Elizabeth pointed out. What was that word that Jessica had used earlier? *Right!* "I've got it. Let's make them call us 'Your Awesomeness.'"

"Perfect!" Mandy exclaimed as she and Mary crowded around Elizabeth to see the paper.

"All girls present at this party shall furthermore be addressed as Your Awesomeness," Elizabeth wrote, "for the period of one week, beginning once this paper is signed." She tore the page out of her notebook and offered it to Bruce. "Sign," she commanded.

Bruce took the paper and the pen. Elizabeth thought he looked pretty silly with his white sheet wrapped around him in some places and torn in others. "I guess we don't have any choice," he muttered, and wrote his name. Then he passed the paper on to Brian.

"No fair signing 'Johnny Buck,'" Elizabeth said, on the lookout for practical jokes.

When all four boys had signed the paper, Elizabeth folded it neatly and placed it on the shelf. "Let's hear it!" she directed.

"Cluck, cluck, cluck," Aaron began softly.

"Louder!" Lila demanded. "I can't hear you!"

"Cluck, cluck, cluck," Bruce chimed in. "Cluck, cluck, cluck, cluck!"

Elizabeth leaned back against the couch and laughed. *I wish I had a movie camera,* she said to herself.

"Can I please have a towel?" Charlie asked when the clucking had been done to the girls' satisfaction.

"You forgot something," Jessica sang out.

Bruce nudged Charlie and whispered something in his ear. Charlie sighed. "Could I please have a towel, Your Awesomeness?" he asked, spitting out the last word as though it had been poisoned.

Elizabeth got up from her seat. "Of course!" she said brightly, wondering whether she should add "Your Chickenness." *Or would "Your Cowardness" sound better?* "In fact, why don't you all stay for a few minutes, till Charlie's all dried off?" she asked.

"Good idea," Jessica told her with a wink. "They can practice our new titles on us. What's my name, boys?"

"Jessica, Your Awesomeness," Brian answered, making a face.

"Tell you what," Jessica said. "Let's even invite the guys to stay and have some hot chocolate with us."

"Sound good?" Maria asked teasingly.

"Yes, Your Awesomeness," they replied together.

*   *   *

This is the best slumber party of my life! Jessica exulted as she went out into the kitchen to get another plate of cookies. *No possible way it could have been any better. No possible way.*

Humming to herself, she stepped into the pantry. She had just picked up a package of chocolate chip cookies when she heard a noise. Plenty of noises were coming from the living room—but this one seemed different. Jessica held still.

No. It wasn't from the living room.

Instead, it seemed to be coming from—yes, that was right—

From downstairs.

In the basement.

The basement, Jessica thought with a shiver of alarm. *But there's no one down in the basement right now—*

Is there?

Ten

"What was that?" Lila squealed.

"I think—I think it's coming from the basement," Elizabeth said nervously, a frown crossing her face.

"What's down in the basement?" Maria asked.

"N-nothing," Elizabeth stammered. All she could think of was rats.

"Oh, come on, you guys!" Bruce pleaded. "I mean, Your Awesomenesses! Don't you think we've had enough tricks for one night?"

"Yeah—aren't you satisfied yet?" Charlie complained. He was wrapped tightly in his towel, but his teeth still chattered.

Amy shot an anxious glance. "Um, this isn't a trick. We didn't plan it."

"Yeah, well, Jessica left the room a minute

ago," Bruce said. "Did she go down there?"

Elizabeth shook her head. "No way. She couldn't have made it down there fast enough." *And she wouldn't do something like that to us, either,* she added to herself.

"Oh, give me a break!" Brian burst out. "There's obviously a logical explanation for this. Do you think we're total fools?"

Elizabeth gritted her teeth. *You don't really want me to answer that.* She fixed Brian with a serious look. "Believe me, Brian. This wasn't in the script."

There was silence for a moment—and then a strange, awful sound from downstairs.

"It sounds like somebody moaning!" Mandy exclaimed in a horrified whisper.

The girls huddled closer together. "Doesn't anyone want to go and investigate?" Elizabeth asked nervously, trying not to think about the Hound of the Baskervilles.

"Well, it's your house, Elizabeth," Janet said sternly.

Elizabeth was about to reply when suddenly the lights flickered. A moment later they went off all over the house—every last one of them.

Jessica had just poured some cookies out onto the plate when the lights went out. She shrank back, her heart in her mouth. "Elizabeth? Is that you?" she tried to call out, hoping it was only some of the girls playing a joke on her. But though her mouth opened, no sound came out.

Frantically Jessica tried to figure out where the living room door was. The kitchen was darker than she could ever remember. All directions seemed the same. *How about going left?* she thought, beginning to feel panicked. She turned left, took a step, and banged right into the edge of the counter. *Oooof!*

The moaning was louder now. *Which way? Which way?* Jessica asked herself. She forced herself to think. If you stood at the counter and faced the windows, then the door to the living room would be—

To the right. Yes, to the right.

Jessica turned around and lunged to the right. Two steps, three. With her hands out in front of her, she groped through the darkness. Four steps, five. *I must be almost there*, she thought in alarm. *How many steps from the counter to the door?* She realized she had no idea.

The moaning continued. Six steps, seven—

"Ow!"

Jessica reached down and grabbed her leg. What had she run into? Her fingers brushed against something hard and wooden. *Oh.*

She was still in the kitchen—all by herself and right next to the stairs.

The moaning from downstairs was getting closer. Louder, too. Jessica could feel the vibrations as whatever-it-was came upstairs. She tried very hard not to think about Bloody Fingers McComish.

There was only one thing to be done. Darting inside the pantry, she slammed the door shut after her.

I wish the candle were still lit, Elizabeth thought in the living room. The room was pitch black.

Unable to see a thing, Elizabeth strained to use all her other senses. Off in a corner of the room Bruce and Lila were clutching each other; she could tell because of the way they both whimpered. Someone's head was pressed up tightly against Elizabeth's knee. She didn't know whose. As for Elizabeth, her own head was thrust up against someone's stomach. It might have been Janet's, but she wasn't sure.

Come to think of it, she wasn't even sure it was a girl's.

The moaning got louder. Footsteps echoed through the house. A door slammed. *That's the door at the top of the basement stairs*, Elizabeth said to herself. She recognized the sound very well. She had slammed that door many times when she and Jessica and Steven were little kids. *I hope we make it to be older kids*, she thought.

The footsteps began again. This time they started coming through the kitchen, echoing against the tiled floor.

Elizabeth's heart thumped. *The kitchen—with Jessica! Oh, Jessica, you're in the kitchen with this—this Thing!*

Elizabeth's mind told her to get up and do something.

But her body wouldn't move.

Almost as soon as the pantry door swung shut, Jessica realized that she had made a terrible mistake. Better to be outside, where she could run if she had to, than inside where it was cramped and crowded. *How could I have thought the kitchen was dark, anyway?* she wondered. *Compared with the pantry it's as bright as a beach.*

Jessica backed up a step. Something made a clanging noise. She swept her arm back to push whatever it was away—and knocked a box off the shelf. Something spilled all over the floor—she could hear it whooshing out. *Spaghetti*, she told herself, trying hard to calm down. *Spaghetti, that's all it is. Just spaghetti. You've seen it a million times.* She thought of the times when she and Elizabeth and Mrs. Wakefield would cook dinner together. Sometimes they would make spaghetti, she remembered. *If I get out of here alive*, she promised herself, *I'll make sure to enjoy those times more.*

Jessica picked up her foot to stretch it. When she put it down again, there was a crackling noise.

Oh, no! It's like bones cracking!

Jessica held her breath. *No, wait—it's only spaghetti again. I stepped on a strand of spaghetti, that's all. Stay calm*, she told herself. *There's nothing to worry about. There's nothing—*

Just then, she heard a noise—and it wasn't the kind of noise spaghetti makes when it's stepped on. The noise wasn't coming from inside the pantry at all, in fact—and it wasn't coming from the basement either. There were footsteps and moaning coming from somewhere in the kitchen. The thing—whatever it was—was probably standing just three feet away from her.

A weapon, that was what she needed. Her heart beating wildly, Jessica felt with her fingers along the shelf nearest her. Could she find a can? She banged into one, but it rolled off the shelf and crashed to the floor. Jessica clamped her hand firmly across her mouth to keep from screaming.

Go away, she pleaded silently. Just go away.

Jessica felt her stomach rumble. *Of all times to be hungry!* she thought. But she had to admit, a pantry was a good place to be trapped in as far as hunger was concerned. Of course, it would be nice to have some light so you could see what you were eating. It wouldn't be much fun to bite into some potato chips and find it was dry oatmeal instead.

It suddenly occurred to Jessica that her predicament was just like what happened to the victim in the Poe story she'd read, "The Cask of Amontillado." At the end of the story, she remembered with a tingle of fear, the man who owned the wine sealed his friend inside the crypt. Forever. He placed bricks in front of the entrance and—

Stop, she ordered herself. *Don't think about it!*

But she couldn't stop. *What if I get bricked in?* she asked herself frantically, wondering if any of those mysterious noises from the other side of the door were the sounds of bricks being put into place. *I can still get out now,* she told herself. All she had to do was push open the door, shove it as hard as she could, and then—

And then she'd be at the mercy of whatever it was.

It's here, Elizabeth realized. The Thing must have crossed through the kitchen. Now it was standing in the doorway to the living room—not more than a few feet away from Elizabeth herself. She strained her eyes. In the dim light that was coming through the window, she could almost make out a figure. Tall.

And terrifying.

A single beam of light pierced the room. Elizabeth gasped. It was headed directly for her. Blinded by the light, she dived even lower and hid her head.

"I'm dead!" Aaron screamed behind her.

"It's got a light ray!" Mandy cried out.

Her heart in her mouth, Elizabeth clutched the person next to her—whoever it was. *Make it go away,* she pleaded. *Just make it go away.* Frightened as she was, though, Elizabeth couldn't keep her eyes off the figure. She could see the light bouncing off the walls and back to the doorway, where it raked up and down the figure. The bouncing light created a strobe effect, but Elizabeth could see well enough to tell that the figure wasn't entirely human. Its face was pale ghostly white, its clothes torn and stained a bloody red, and its chest—

Its chest, Elizabeth told herself, feeling slightly sick, *its chest has a bloody knife sticking right out of it*.

At least it wasn't a hound.

Elizabeth scampered over to the windows, as far from the creature as she could get. She could hear Lila and Bruce screaming, and she could tell that she was screaming too—though she couldn't remember when she'd begun. Could she break the window behind her if she had to?

The Thing was coming forward, flashing the light all around the room, laughing maniacally now.

Will I ever see anyone again? Elizabeth asked herself, hearing Lila start to sob next to her. *I wish I could say good-bye to my family—Jessica and Mom and Dad—and I'm sorry for all the arguing I've done with everyone—Jessica and Steven, especially, and—*

Wait a minute.

Elizabeth pricked up her ears. That creature had an awfully familiar laugh, didn't it? She jumped to her feet.

"Steven!" she cried.

*　　　*　　　*

"Ha! Scared you, huh?" Steven exclaimed, his eyes still gleaming, after he'd turned the power back on.

Elizabeth cleared her throat. "Well, kind of," she admitted. Her hands were still shaking. She couldn't remember ever being any more terrified—but she didn't see any reason to tell her brother that.

"That is some costume," Charlie said admiringly. Elizabeth noticed that his cheeks were still a bit pale. "What did you put all over your face, anyway?"

"Secret recipe, kid," Steven said loftily. "When you've been in the business as long as I have—"

Elizabeth rolled her eyes. *Oh, well, let him gloat,* she told herself. She had to admit that his costume was terrifying. Steven had wrapped a piece of cardboard in aluminum foil, covered it with ketchup stains, and stuck it onto his chest to look like a huge bloody knife.

"It looks pretty scary even in the light, doesn't it?" Steven boasted. "It took me hours to get it exactly right. Anyone want to try it on?"

Janet shrieked.

Lila wrapped her arms around herself.

Everybody shrank back.

"Hey, I took a bath today!" Steven said with a chuckle. "Well, OK, then. Anyone want to hear the moan?"

"No, thanks," Elizabeth said with a grimace.

"What was that fright—I mean, that *light*, anyway?"

Steven grinned and showed her—a flashlight.

"A flashlight?" Elizabeth said meekly, feeling foolish.

"A flashlight in the hands of a master!" Steven affirmed.

"I guess it's true what Mr. Bowman said," Maria remarked with a smile. "The old familiar things can be more frightening than new stuff."

At that moment, Jessica appeared behind her brother.

"Jess!" Elizabeth exclaimed. "Are you OK?"

But Jessica didn't answer her. She was staring at Steven, breathing hard. "It was you! I thought—I thought—well, I don't know what I thought."

"Steven gets even!" Steven boasted, shaking hands with himself above his head like a heavyweight boxer.

"I wasn't scared," Janet announced from her position on the edge of the circle. "I knew it was you all the time."

"Yeah, right," Charlie said. "No offense or anything, Janet, but you were trying to hide your head under my leg the whole time. Admit it."

"What are you talking about?" Janet sputtered. "It wasn't me that was under your leg, it was Lila!"

"That's funny," Maria whispered to Elizabeth with a giggle. "I thought Lila was at the window the whole time, screaming her head off."

"Anyway," Charlie said, making sure he had

everyone's attention, "I'd just like to point out that you girls were as scared as us boys."

"Probably even more scared," Brian said.

Mandy snickered. "I wouldn't talk if I were you, Brian," she told him. "You were right next to me the whole time. Should I tell everybody else what you were doing?" Her eyes twinkled.

"OK, OK," Brian said quickly. "At least as scared. But I think we probably ought to call a truce."

"A truce?" Janet scoffed. "Don't give me that. You boys are just cowards, that's all. And by the way, Brian, you forgot to call Mandy 'Your Awesomeness.'"

"Hey, I mean it!" Charlie said. "You girls aren't any braver. You should have seen the look on Lila's face when Steven came into the room."

"Who, me?" Lila retorted. "How would you know, big shot?" She glared at him. "It wasn't like there was enough light to see."

Charlie stepped forward. "There was enough—"

"People, people! May I have your attention, please!" Steven's voice boomed over the squabble. Instantly Charlie and Lila were silent. "I'd like to point out," Steven continued with an exaggerated bow, "that you guys are *all* cowards." Charlie started to say something, but Steven quieted him with a look. "*I* was the man of the hour. Gonna getcha," he sang, imitating Johnny Buck. "Gonna getcha, gonna getcha—Gotcha!"

Elizabeth and Jessica exchanged glances. "No fair," Jessica told Steven. "You didn't give us time to cover our ears."

"I guess I should get those cookies," Jessica said a few minutes later. She hesitated. "Or maybe someone else would like to get them instead?"

"No, thanks," Elizabeth said sleepily. Steven yawned and shook his head.

Jessica wrinkled her nose in frustration. "Well, would you come with me, Lila, please? I mean, I don't think I should have to carry the cookies all by myself."

Lila looked up, startled. "Well—OK," she said hesitantly. "That is, if Janet will come too."

Jessica turned to her sister. "I really think you should come with us, Lizzie. It'll be fun."

Elizabeth grinned. "Oh, all right," she said, getting to her feet. "Tell you what. Maria, Amy, why don't you guys come on in, too—just for old times' sake?"

Jessica laughed. Together the six girls walked into the kitchen. "There's a lot more room here than in that little bathroom," Maria pointed out, leaning against the counter.

"And a good thing, too," Jessica muttered.

"Well, I know what my report will be about!" Elizabeth announced.

"What report?" Jessica asked, picking up the plate.

"My report for English class," Elizabeth explained. "Remember, Mr. Bowman assigned us to do a project about the book we read?"

"Oh, right," Jessica said. She and Amy began to arrange the cookies on the plate. "Thanks for the reminder. So what are you going to do?"

Elizabeth's eyes danced. "I'll write about how we used *The Hound of the Baskervilles* to pull off a scare of our own."

Jessica smiled brightly. "*Great* idea! The boys will be totally humiliated!"

"Actually, I wasn't planning on using any names," Elizabeth told her. "You think I want to begin a whole new Scare War all over again?"

Jessica giggled. "I think I'll tell the story of 'The Cask of Amontillado' again, only it'll be from the point of view of the man who was bricked up inside." She looked at the pantry and shuddered. "I'm kind of an expert on that sort of thing, if you know what I mean."

"Thanks for the hot chocolate and everything," Charlie told the girls about twenty minutes later, "but I think we'd better go."

"We should do this again," Elizabeth said with a grin.

"Yeah, right," Brian said, rolling his eyes.

The girls all accompanied the boys to the front door. It was a warm night, with patches of fog here and there now that the rain had stopped. Elizabeth breathed in the air. She loved the way the world smelled after a rainstorm.

Charlie grimaced. "It's pretty foggy out there," he muttered.

Jessica shot him a sideways glance. "You're not scared, are you?"

Charlie swallowed hard and looked at the other boys. "No way," he said bravely. "Scared? You've got to be kidding."

Elizabeth looked around. The fog made it a perfect night for a scare or a mystery. *Luckily,* she found herself thinking, *we've had more than enough scares this week to last us a lifetime.*

"Well," Charlie said, walking down the steps, "we're taking off."

"Good night, you guys," Elizabeth called out.

"Good—hey!" Brian's voice suddenly dropped, and he pointed off into the distance. "What's that?"

"Aaaaah!" Charlie screeched suddenly.

"Aaaaah!" Aaron echoed him. Horrified, the four boys ran back up the steps and plowed into Amy and Maria.

Peering out into the mist, Elizabeth gasped. Coming toward her were two terrifying figures.

This is no joke, she told herself, catching a glimpse of two frightening, bloodied faces, half-covered by capes. *This is worse than Steven, worse than the Hound of the Baskervilles—worse than anything!*

"Oh, help!" Elizabeth cried, dashing frantically for the patio before the creatures could get her.

*　　*　　*

Oh, my gosh! Jessica thought in a panic. She couldn't bear to look at the two horrible monsters—but she also couldn't seem to tear her eyes away from them. One had a pale forehead that seemed to shimmer in the darkness, and awful yellow fangs with something stuck to them. *Its dinner?* she wondered. The other seemed to have no face at all. Its eyes were blackened. One was falling out of its socket. Where its nose should have been, there was a gaping, bloody hole—and what appeared to be a hairy spider. Jessica pressed her body up against the front door, wishing she were invisible.

The worst part was, Jessica was all alone—everyone else had managed to escape. Elizabeth was up the tree in the backyard. Janet and Lila had gotten into the house and slammed the door before she had made it inside herself. She knew one or two of the boys had reached the patio, and a lot of kids were hiding in the bushes, far away from these two evil grinning monsters that were coming to get her. And Steven—

Steven, she thought with a sudden surge of hope. Maybe it was one of his jokes. But it couldn't be. She remembered having seen him run off into the sun porch.

Jessica's heart felt ready to explode. She shrank back, feeling for a crack in the wall. She could hear Janet and Lila screaming on the other side of the door. "Let me in!" She knocked desperately against the door. "Let me in!" But there was no response from inside.

Jessica watched in terror as the creatures came closer—

The two shadowy figures clapped each other on the back. Then, to Jessica's astonishment, they shook hands.

"Hi, kids!" a familiar voice shouted.

"Hope you had a restful party!" the other monster chimed in.

Jessica drew in her breath and stared. "Mom and Dad," she said softly as the two figures removed their masks.

"Hi, sweetie," Mrs. Wakefield said. "Are you OK? You look a little surprised to see us."

"But you—I don't see—" Jessica stammered.

"Just a little prank," Mr. Wakefield explained. "You're not scared, are you?"

"We figured that kids today are way too sophisticated to be scared by little things like this," Mrs. Wakefield added, tapping her black hood. "So we thought we'd dress up for a few laughs! Hysterical, right?"

"Mmm." Jessica swallowed an enormous bite of her chocolate chip cookie. All the party guests had gone home, and the twins were in the kitchen, having a late-night junk food snack. "Next slumber party let's skip the scary part, and just eat cookies!"

Elizabeth laughed. "Don't you think you'd get a

little sick of cookies if you had to eat them all night?"

"No way!" Jessica insisted. "I'd never ever get sick of cookies. In fact, I'd eat cookies and stuff all day long if I could!"

*What will it take to make Jessica sick of cookies? Find out in Sweet Valley Twins #89, **Jessica's Cookie Disaster**.*

Bantam Books in the SWEET VALLEY TWINS series.
Ask your bookseller for the books you have missed.

SIGN UP FOR THE SWEET VALLEY HIGH® FAN CLUB!

Hey, girls! Get all the gossip on Sweet Valley High's® most popular teenagers when you join our fantastic Fan Club! As a member, you'll get all of this really cool stuff:

- Membership Card with your own personal Fan Club ID number
- A Sweet Valley High® Secret Treasure Box
- Sweet Valley High® Stationery
- Official Fan Club Pencil (for secret note writing!)
- Three Bookmarks
- A "Members Only" Door Hanger
- Two Skeins of J. & P. Coats® Embroidery Floss with flower barrette instruction leaflet
- Two editions of *The Oracle* newsletter
- Plus exclusive Sweet Valley High® product offers, special savings, contests, and much more!

Be the first to find out what Jessica & Elizabeth Wakefield are up to by joining the Sweet Valley High® Fan Club for the one-year membership fee of only $6.25 each for U.S. residents, $8.25 for Canadian residents (U.S. currency). Includes shipping & handling.

Send a check or money order (do not send cash) made payable to "Sweet Valley High® Fan Club" along with this form to:

SWEET VALLEY HIGH® FAN CLUB, BOX 3919-B, SCHAUMBURG, IL 60168-3919

NAME _____
(Please print clearly)

ADDRESS _____

CITY_____ STATE _____ ZIP_____
(Required)

AGE _____ BIRTHDAY_____ /_____ /_____

Offer good while supplies last. Allow 6-8 weeks after check clearance for delivery. Addresses without ZIP codes cannot be honored. Offer good in USA & Canada only. Void where prohibited by law.
©1993 by Francine Pascal   LCI-1383-123